# KESTREL VS. THE ILLUMINATI

## A Kestrel Investigates select your own adventure book

Oliver Semple

*This book is dedicated to my eldest brother James,
for your endless encouragement, I thank you.*

# FOREWORD

I first met Oliver Semple on his feature film, Kenneth, in which I played the evil Ear Goblin. I knew that Oliver and I would get along as soon as I read the script (co-written with Anthony Farren) and saw the direction: "Then blood comes out of his ear (just like in Star Trek II: The Wrath of Khan)." Sure enough, when filming began in June 2010, we did get along.

Kenneth was a special project for me; the kind of film I would want to watch, even if I wasn't in it. A metaphorical representation of the inner demons we all must face in life, I was drawn to both its caustic humour and underlying human warmth—both of which are emblematic of Oliver's writing. (If you haven't seen Kenneth yet, it's now available to watch for free on YouTube.)

When the film premiered at Edinburgh's Bootleg Film Festival in 2013, Oliver and Anthony quite rightly won the Best Screenplay Award, but mooted follow-ups (including one in which I was to play a gun-toting creature who thought he was Roy Orbison) failed to materialise. In late-2017, however, I received a text from Oliver asking if I would like to play a hapless paranormal investigator called Agravain Kestrel. Of course I would!

A multi-episode YouTube series, Kestrel Investigates would be less ambitious (i.e. less expensive) than gun-toting Roy Orbison-monsters and would make good use of Yorkshire locations (another hallmark of Oliver's film work)—albeit, usually filmed in the dead of winter, in the middle of the night. As well as directing, Oliver took on the role of Kestrel's cynical cameraman,

Mike. In some ways, the characters are distorted reflections of our own personalities—although not as credulous as Kestrel, I share a lifelong interest and belief in the paranormal, while Oliver is definitely more sceptical.

We filmed the first episode, "The Owlman of Pontefract", in January 2018. Since then, we have encountered many things that go bump in the night, including a Poppleton Witch, a Wetwang Vampire, a Screaming Skull, and even Santa Claus. We have shared "Close Encounters of the Thirsk Kind"; visited "The Temple of the Horned God"; and, in "The Haunted Shed", I was possessed by the spirit of Wakefield's foremost Freddie Mercury impersonator. All of which leads us here, to what must be the first ever Choose Your Own Adventure book to have been sired by a YouTube series.

As Oliver and I are both children of the 1980s, we grew up reading gamebooks, especially Steve Jackson and Ian Livingstone's Fighting Fantasy series (Oliver's growing collection of which makes me feel less guilty about reliving my own childhood through amassing Doctor Who Target novelisations). My personal favourites were those CYOA titles published by Bantam, like The Cave of Time, Vampire Express and The Deadly Shadow—although I often gave up after I had been "deaded" once. Hopefully, you will be more persistent with Kestrel vs. the Illuminati, in which you, too, can take on the role of York's leading "professional paranormal enthusiast" and battle the dark forces that control our world.

I hope you enjoy it, and I hope to see you all on some new investigations in the near future.

Love and mercy,

Stephen Mosley

# PREFACE

One day I was twirling around in my chair, winding down a mid-management position in a large insurance company, killing time to claim a small amount of redundancy money when an idea struck me. In the mid-nineties there was a program called 'Fortean TV' - why don't I make a parody of it!? It was a fleeting idea but it only fleeted so far and kept fleeting back and forth inside my head until I decided to do something about it.

 Initially I was going to set the program in the nineties until a friend (Anthony Farren) suggested it should be set in modern times and based on YouTube. Well, the stage was set, a random name generator threw up the name Agravain Kestrel, we liked it, we kept it and before long we had a title for the show.

 Once finally released from my dead end job I wrote the first six episodes in six days and on the sabbath, I rested. That became the first series. We filmed it in early 2018 and my head exploded with more ideas for future episodes, the potential for the show seemed endless and as I wrote series two and then three (not yet filmed) the 'Kestrel Universe' expanded.
During this period I was replaying Fighting Fantasy books from my youth and figured 'huh, I wonder if anyone has ever written a comedy choose your own adventure book?' - it turns out they have, but I didn't let that deter me!

 So here it is, after much procrastination and many large pieces of paper with confusing spider diagrams, the first and possibly last Kestrel select your own adventure book.

You will die, but hopefully it will make you laugh.

Oliver Semple.

The red light flashes on. The faceless person behind the camera silently counts you in with his fingers: five, four, three, two, one! Lifting the microphone to your mouth you introduce yourself to the viewers with boyish enthusiasm "Hello and welcome, I am Agravain Kestrel, professional paranormal enthusiast. Behind the camera is my good friend Mike, say hello Mike." The person behind the camera doesn't respond, you try to focus on his dark silhouette but the more you concentrate, the more it spreads and dissipates. You look down to your hands and realise the microphone is no longer there, looking past your hands to the ground you see far below you a congregation of hooded people standing in a circle and in the middle is a tall man with a top hat who talks far too loudly. You watch the audience through the eyes of the tall man, watching their half-covered faces contort with expressions of excitement, rage and disgust. Within the circle a teenage boy band appear from nowhere, singing and dancing, your hand reaches out in front of you with its thumb pointing downwards. Fire erupts all around and you fall back into a chair. In front of you a computer monitor shows your most recent Kestrel Investigates YouTube video 'The Dancing Dog of Tadcaster', the view counter spins constantly, 1 million views, 2 million views, 3 million views. Outside the house people are peering into your windows, clamouring for your attention, your front door explodes open, you rush toward the doorway and are greeted with a blinding light and an incredibly loud beeping noise.

Turn to 1.

# 1

Beep beep beep!

You are startled awake by the sound of your alarm clock at the ungodly hour of 9:30am. The vivid emotions stirred up by your dreams quickly melt away like frost in the morning sun, replaced by the usual feeling of sad resignation when you realise YOU ARE AGRAVAIN KESTREL. You feel tired and filled with regret, as enjoyable as it seemed at the time watching YouTube videos of funny dogs until 4am now doesn't seem like a good idea. What a fool you've been, you know fine well that it is your fortnightly inquisition at the job centre this morning at 11am. Lying there, the incessant beeping of your alarm clock echoes in your ears. The weight of responsibility crushes you into the mattress, you gauge your anxiety levels and...

Turn off the alarm and get up to face the music (turn to 57)

Decide that nine more minutes of fretting will help and snooze the alarm (turn to 112)

Turn off the alarm entirely, curl up into the foetal position and re-enter the land of nod (turn to 51)

## 2

Behind the counter a middle-aged woman angrily stamps and stacks books, you approach and stand there quietly waiting for her to look up and notice you. After ten minutes you gently clear your throat prompting the librarian to emit a loud exasperated sigh as she rolls her eyes in your direction.

You explain that your library card has expired (more loud sighs, eye rolls and an echoing tut) and you wish to renew it, she snatches your old card out of your sweaty hand, scrutinises it one inch away from her spectacle lens and then chops it in half with some scissors.

"Your new card will cost five pounds." she barks, then returns to stamping the living daylights out of some books.

If you have a five pound note (turn to 58)

If you don't have a five pound note (turn to 99)

# 3

Ever since secondary school the sound of other people's laughter makes you instantly paranoid, but being the curious little hedgehog that you are, the laughter still reels you in. As you approach further, twisting your way down the winding tunnel you see a flickering, colourful light and the noise of a television set. Rounding the final corner you peek your squinting, myopic eyes out into a darkened room, which you now see is dominated by a large, vulgar flat-screen TV, bolted onto the wall. In front of the entertaining slab is a sofa and on the sofa sits a fat man who is guffawing loudly at the content being jizzed out by the telly.

You struggle to make sense of the program currently being shown, which appears to have a man dressed as an old, Irish

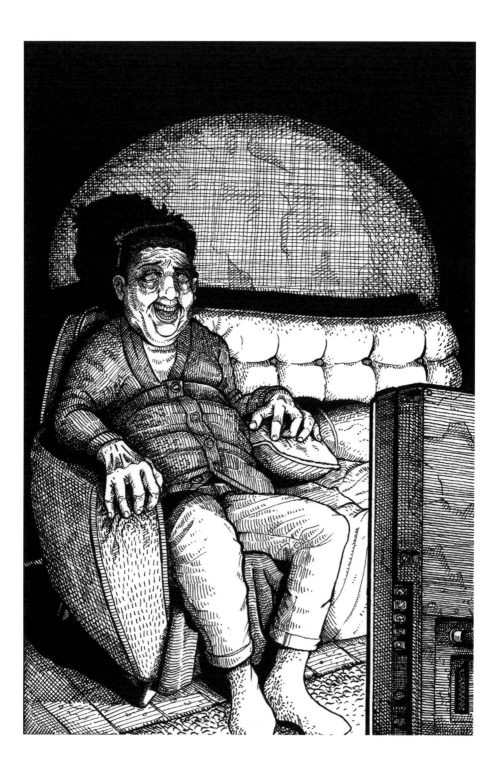

woman in her kitchen who makes crass jokes amongst a parade of unlikeable fools. Regardless of what you think the chubby viewer continues to scream with laughter every time a sexual double entendre is uttered or some trousers fall down. Moving slowly around the room you are able to see the man's face, it is twisted and contorted by the laughter. He looks at you and you are shocked to see nothing but pain and terror in his gaze, his eyes beg you for help and you can see now how he desperately gasps for air in between his spasmodic chuckles. You beckon Mike over and he immediately starts to deride the program, then sits down on the sofa. As soon as Mike's bottom touches the cushion his face lights up and his head cocks towards the TV screen, involuntarily barking harsh laughter. Being an idiot you fail to make

the connection between the sofa and whatever evil curse is at play here, so you sit next to Mike to try and shake him out of it – instantly you are pulled back by an unseen force into a viewing position and like Mike and the unfortunate corpulent man, you now begin to cackle loudly.

After roughly 48 hours of exhausting laughter the effort takes it's toll and Mike is the first to die, his organs (already weakened by years of alcohol and cocodamol abuse) shutting down from over exertion. Mike's death is followed swiftly by the demise of the unknown chubby guy and finally within another day you also expire on the sofa.

You are dead.

**4**

Wulf, being a native of Germany, cannot cope with your emotional eruption. He hurriedly asks you to sign on the dotted line, assures you everything will be alright in an uncaring tone, slips a fiver into your hand and ushers you towards glorious freedom.

YOU HAVE PICKED UP THE FIVE POUND NOTE.

You emerge from the Job Centre, stepping over the dead and dying clogging the exit and stumble back onto the mean streets of York. Eyes red and bleary from your pathetic outburst and with five pounds scorching a hole in your pocket you set off to celebrate another fortnight of living beneath the bread line.

With directionless enthusiasm you set off at pace not knowing where your feet might whisk you, walking halfway down the street, doubling back then eventually just standing there looking gormless. How should a carefree, cash-rich bachelor spend such a fine day?

Go back home and see if Mike wants to play 'flick the light switch off with a tea towel' (turn to 23)

Go back to 'Journeyman' comic book shop to see if the unknown person is still signing the whatever (turn to 124)

Have a wander over to Waitrose with your newfound wealth to see how the other half live (turn to 87)

14

## 5

Option two takes you to yet another line of hissing and clicking noises only this time you can tell it is being aggressive. You begin to argue with the recorded message, quickly losing and then wait until it has finished admonishing you in its unfamiliar tongue. After ten minutes your patience is starting to wear thin and your ear is becoming uncomfortably warm, you decide enough is enough!

Turn to 121.

## 6

The dog is quite quick but you manage to keep up the pace as it darts through streets, across busy roads and out of the bustling city centre into the rural suburbs. Caught up in the excitement of tracking this mysterious animal you step off a kerb clumsily and manage to twist your ankle, falling heavily onto the tarmac like a sleeping bag full of tellys. Using every ounce of your atrophied upper body strength you manage to haul yourself onto a small wall and are surprised when the dog you had been following doubles back and approaches you dragging a sturdy stick, shaped like a Y at one end like a perfect crutch. You marvel at this and decide a dog this clever needs an appropriate name, a name that signifies its intelligence, so you call it Stephen Fry. Heartened by Stephen Fry's assistance you push yourself back to your feet, Stephen Fry bites your trouser leg and pulls, then sets back off in the direction he was originally heading, he clearly wants you to follow so you hobble after him.

Turn to 44.

## 7

A cold, lisping recorded voice answers and rapidly begins to list some options:

Option one: If you are not a member and know nothing about whom we are or what we do then press one (turn to 102)

Option two: To hear these options in Alpha Draconian press two (turn to 79)

Option three: If you are calling to receive your orders press three (turn to 94)

If you get sick of listening to the options and decide to go to the address listed on the card (turn to 119)

## 8

You politely decline, citing your reasons. Peter nods understandingly and explains that you can no longer bear witness to the clubs mysterious ceremony if you are not willing to participate. He asks for one of his club members to escort you away and gives you a polite smile as you are ushered down a corridor.

The light grows dim as you continue down the stone passage, your guide advises you to step forward into a waiting elevator.

"Don't worry, you don't have to press any buttons." he explains and closes the door behind you.

For fifteen minutes you stand there in the pitch black waiting to for the elevator to move but nothing happens. Turning around to look for an emergency button you feel the walls and realise they are made of stone, your hands run across the door and feel metal bars. This is not a lift, it's a cell.

Hours pass, you fall asleep.

Turn to 125.

# 9

Approaching the Job Centre door through a miasma of cigarette smoke and despair, the familiar panic washes over you as you realise you have not prepared your fortnightly excuses. Your designated scrutiniser, a joyless drone named Wulf, glimpses you through a sea of staggering addicts and beckons your name. Like an antelope singled out for destruction by a predator on the plains of the Serengeti your fight or flight mechanism kicks in hard.

Approach your Employment Specialist 'Wulf Schmidt', man up and sit down (turn to 83)

Let out a high pitched shriek and run screaming from the building (turn to 108)

## 10

Using the reflexes gained from a virtual lifetime of martial arts the monocular homunculus leads you a merry dance around Argos, from the counter, to the entrance and back to the bit with the little sheets of paper and impractically short biros. Eventually you managed to catch it in a display of military grade water pistols and walk towards the exit still staring at your phone screen, pleased at a job well done. On your way out you miss the step and badly jar your lower back, instantly sending your lumbar region into spasm. Shoppers tut and curse you as they are forced to step over your juddering body that is blocking the shops entrance. After forty-five minutes the manager comes and with the assistance of his staff move you out onto the pavement.

You awake in hospital with a taxi bill for forty-five quid stapled to your jacket and spend the next month of your life in bed on a concoction of strong painkillers and muscle relaxants deliriously bankrupting yourself through the eBay app on your phone.

Your adventure ends here.

## 11

Panting heavily, you plough your way through the coronavirus-riddled, tourist-packed streets of York, your Lynx Africa deodorant showing itself to be woefully not fit for purpose. As usual the outside world is loud and confusing, big issue sellers yell, cyclists whizz past and pigeons do that annoying thing where they suddenly appear and flap about at chest height. You head down Goodramgate and whilst walking past the local comic book shop 'Journeyman' you notice a book signing is in progress, your watch states you have ten minutes to spare.

Remind yourself you cannot afford a new anything and keep walking to the Job Centre (turn to 9)

Give in to your excitement to go inside the shop to see who is signing what (turn to 124)

## 12

Wulf listens to your lies with a barely concealed, growing impatience. You keep talking wondering when he is going to interject but he allows you to continue, giving you enough rope to hang yourself with several times over. After five full minutes of desperate fantasy you find yourself talking about the malnourished cat with one eye that lives on your street that has no collar and asking Wulf if he thinks you should call the RSPCA, your question hangs in the air for twenty or so excruciating seconds before Wulf finally opens his mouth to tell you he is stopping your benefits. He stamps your little book and hands it back to you, explaining that over the twelve years he has worked there he has never heard such obvious porkie pies. Desperation hits and out of sheer panic you ask if there are any jobs going here, he replies yes and asks if you want an application form. Frightened that you might actually be heading towards employment you back pedal frantically, declining the form and telling him you will apply later online then leave the Job Centre knowing full well you won't. Heading back into town you go past the comic book shop 'Journeyman' and see that there is some sort of book signing happening. Your interest well and truly piqued you decide to go in.

Turn to 124.

## 13

You walk alongside the river until the fearsome candyfloss beast appears. You throw several 'Jabaguy' orbs at it in order it to capture it but each time you do it turns around and deflects the orb with a huge pink buttock. After roughly twenty attempts the creature winks, blows a kiss and vanishes causing you to throw a tantrum so wild that you lose your balance and fall into the River Ouse. Despite being a strong swimmer the current drags you under time and time again as your body is swept downstream. As you manage to make it back to the surface you try to use your phone to ring the emergency services but the water has damaged the handheld item and as a result the screen is stuck on a loop of the winking pink 'Jabaguy'. As the water fills your lungs and you lose consciousness your last sight in this world is that fluffy, pink grotesque blowing a kiss.

Two months later your badly decomposed body is found near Naburn Mariner, detectives working on the case review your life and assume you were a suicide.


You are dead.

# 14

For you the magic of the cinema has never worn off, each time you sit in those hallowed seats you are still gripped with excitement, be it from the special effects, the enthralling storylines or what the next Revel might be. With these thoughts in your mind you happily stroll into the multiplex, the smell of warm popcorn filling your nostrils as you glance at the different films on offer. There are three that take your fancy: a Sci-Fi comedy called 'Help, My mom is a time travelling, zombie, alien vampire', the new Bond film 'Live and Let Live' in which the secret agent is played by an old, black, transsexual actor so as not to offend anyone and finally an unnecessary remake of 'Planes, Train and Automobiles' starring 50 cent and Will Ferrell.

After thirty minutes of deliberating the decision is made for you as two of the films have already started. You aren't going to be 'that guy' who stumbles around in the dark once the film has already begun, so you 'choose' the new Bond film and it isn't until you get to the counter that you remember you haven't got two pennies to rub together. What do you do:

Go outside the cinema and ask the busker who is currently murdering 'Moonlight Shadow' if he can spare five quid (turn to 49)

Use all of your stealth and cunning built up from years of playing hide and seek to try and sneak into the showing?(turn to 54)

Wait around in the foyer, looking lost and frightened, hoping a real adult will come along and fix your problem (turn to 117)

## 15

You must act quick as Mike is being overpowered by the powerhouse entertainment duo lookalikes, the only thing to do is attack Peter, but with what – you have no weapons. Mike cries out in pain as one of his attackers pulls his hair, his agonising shriek propels you into battle and you run straight at Peter, fists clenched and arms wheeling around in great circles. Peter, being so stupidly tall, extends his arm and halts your progress by placing his hand on your scalp. Eyes closed, spit foaming on your lips you swing wildly and ineffectively at the giant until he pushes you back and with a spartan style kick, hoofs you in the chest, breaking your rib cage and sending you into cardiac arrest.

As your chest tightens and your life energy leaves your body you overhear someone in the crowd say 'Kestrel Investigates – you won't have seen it, it's a shit webseries.'

You are dead.

## 16

From within your coat pocket you pull out the half eaten bag of jelly sweets you found in the cinema. As the ceremony continues you scoff the entire bag of sweets like the greedy pig you are, if you were able to get an NHS dentist they would be so disappointed in you. Mike shakes his head and fixes you with a gaze of pure disgust.

Turn to 98.

## 17

The window rattles wildly with every throb of the buses engine, your spectacles make a high pitched buzzing noise whenever the corner of the frame comes into contact with the glass. Gradually the rhythmic pulse makes you sleepy and your eyelids become heavier and heavier until finally they shut. Drool pours from your mouth and down the pane as your mind relaxes and soothing thoughts begin to permeate your grey matter. You float, adrift in an ocean of nothingness. Outside your mind the bus continues onward past your stop and many others until finally it reaches the end of the line.

You are awoken from your gentle slumber by the driver's fat hand violently rocking you back and forth, the window is no longer vibrating and the bus is stationary. Outside the window the world is grey and filtered through a thick curtain of drizzle. People shuffle past wearing expressions of defeat, pound shops litter the high street, a dog lies down in a puddle and willingly drowns itself. Disorientated you ask the driver '"What fresh hell is this?" and his response send shivers of terror down your spine. You have suffered a fate worse than death, you have accidentally got the bus to Doncaster.


Your adventure ends here.

## 18

You check your phone credit before calling and discover that you have precisely sixty-eight pence remaining, if you are going to make this call you will need to 'top up'. The thought of using your bank card brings you out in a cold sweat, you have been plumbing the depths of an increased overdraft with a buffer and you know the end is nigh. Going through the options you slowly add your card number and wait for what seems like an eternity until an automated voice states 'payment is complete, you now have ten pounds and sixty eight pence credit'. Recovering from the shock that your bank card worked, you type in the number from the back of the golden business card and the phone begins to ring.

Turn to 7.

## 19

As you emerge back onto the cobbled streets the sunlight forces you into the shadows like a nocturnal rodent, your beady eye-balls stream from the bright light which also causes you to make a revolting snuffling noise. Pedestrians give you a wide berth and seem terrified when you make eye contact with them, especially the women - but then that's no different to normal. Cowering in a urine-soaked street corner outside of Tesco express you know you must get moving, but which way:

Go Left (turn to 29)

Go straight forward (turn to 96)

Go Right (turn to 80)

## 20

You enter the Library and the impressive Victorian architecture immediately instils you with a sense of order and authority. Introverts silently shuffle around the building, foreign students huddle in groups at tables, students and the unemployed access the internet to send free text messages and check their emails.

You've always loved the Library for many reasons, the chief one being that everything is free, you can take out books to read or better still take home DVDs and CDs then pirate them. Stroking your chin to aid thought you wonder which section you should visit today:

Books (Sci-Fi and Horror) (turn to 36)

DVDs (Sci-Fi and Horror) (turn to 85)

Music (Country and Western) (turn to 95)

## 21

Once you approach the 'Jabaguy's' location it quickly becomes apparent that this circular electrical beastie is hiding in a private residence and without breaking and entering you are never going to get close enough to capture it. Around the side of the house you manage to open a gate and get within spitting distance of your quarry, noticing a small open window at the top of the kitchen window frame you lean in your hands and arms but are unable to see, so you are forced to put your head inside too. You manage to engage the creature and are about to throw your first 'Jaba-guy' orb when you notice a large, shocked man sitting at a breakfast bar, mouth agape and dripping half masticated shreddies. You clumsily yank yourself back out through the window, sprint down the side passage and to freedom, your thighs chafing with every stride. Finally, after forty-five seconds of pure exertion you find yourself wandering back into the city centre and towards the library.

You put away your phone and head towards the entrance of the library but as you do an old homeless woman crosses your path shaking a cardboard cup in your direction. Your hands automatically pat your pockets in the international sign of 'leave me alone' and continue to walk past her into the library.

Turn to 20.

## 22

After you press for option 1 you hear an english voice say 'please hold the line, you are being connected'. The phone rings in a different tone to before and you continue to wait until a recorded message comes on 'Welcome to the British Broadcasting Corporation, please hold'. Suddenly the phone is answered and a hissing voice is heard on the other side, you panic and say hello, there is a pause.

A female voice answers and asks "Who is speaking please?" You decide that your mother didn't raise no liar so you tell them, it is Agravain Kestrel. The unknown voice on the phone ruminates for a moment and then asks how you got this number, after much discussion you fill them in and they invite you to meet them in a local coffee shop so they can explain all about their special club and how you can join.

You arrive predictably late and a woman is already waiting there for you wearing sunglasses and a long leather coat, when she greets you it becomes obvious she is the lady you were speaking to you on the phone. She shakes your hand and leads you into the coffee shop, buys you a drink and gets you the table with the comfy chairs – you imagine this is what is must be like to be on a date and you like it.

"Tell me about yourself." The kind lady asks, so you fill her in with the relevant details – you are thirty seven, on a long term career break, not currently in a relationship etc, she smiles as you talk and drink your coffee. Before long the caffeine has a predicatble effect and you excuse yourself to the little boys room. As you enter the toilet cubicle the woman walks in behind you and wedges the door shut, you stare at her in disbelief as she begins to unbutton her coat.

"Turn around." she whispers and you comply (more out of politeness than anything) when suddenly she pulls out a screwdriver and plunges it into the back of your neck, waggling it around to fully sever your spinal cord.

You are dead.

## 23

Mike isn't at home when you get there so you collapse in a funky heap onto the sofa, there is no point playing 'Switch-whipping' on your own, besides your legs are tired from walking, you are much more suited to sitting these days.

In a perfect world cups of tea would make themselves but sadly this isn't 'Star Trek - The Next Generation' and replicator technology is still at least ten years away so you are forced to get up and go to the kitchen. You manage to find a clean mug as the kettle boils and you mash your teabag with a whisk (the only clean implement in the kitchen) before reaching into the fridge for milk, horrified to find Mike has used it all on his crunchy nuts! Again!

As if life couldn't get any worse you are forced to walk to the little shops, to break into your fiver and buy some more milk. It is always a calculated risk to visit your local shops as there are usually truant teenagers hanging around, waiting to prey on vulnerable adults like yourself, but needs must as the devil drives so you head out on your dangerous errand.

Sure as eggs is eggs, the shop is infested with rodent-faced, tracksuit-wearing teens, walking around with their hands down the front of their jogging pants as if their genitals were a fan heater. They spot you immediately and watch as you pick up some milk and move over to the counter to buy it. You make your procurement and head out of the shop, heart hammering in your chest from adrenaline, you hope you have made it out of there without incident but within a few metres of the exit you hear the familiar drawl of the Yorkshire scally behind you.

"Ere mate, borrow us a quid!" shouts one of the urchins, you respond weakly by telling them you don't have any money, but this blatant lie doesn't quite cut the mustard. The largest hoodlum walks up to you and challenges your response directly.

"You what dickhead?" he says, spraying strawberry vape-smelling spit in your face "I saw you put your fucking change in your pocket. Gimme all your money or I'll bop ya!"

You dutifully hand over your money as instructed by your teenage mugger and walk away (your testosterone levels plummeting below pre-puberty levels) in the wrong direction to your house. In order to get home you'd have to walk past the scallies again or take a mile long detour, so you head off on the detour. Shortly after setting off you forget where you are going and end up back in town, you sit on a bench feeling frustrated by your lack of concentration and… hey look! A cute, stray dog! Let's follow it!

Turn to 6.

## 24

Shaking with anger you join the long queue to meet Russell Bland. One by one the line shuffles along and your mind drifts as you eye the shelves that groan with all the board games you would love to play if you had the money/space/time/friends/ability to understand rules. Halfway down the line an hour has passed when Russell stands up and calls 'Lunchy time', his irritating voice and mannerisms top up your hatred and you refocus your animosity. You patiently stand for the next hour and forty five minutes until Russell reappears, skinny latte in hand and resumes his position at the signing table, all the while your mind struggles to decide upon exactly what you will say when you reach him. Indecision leads to anxiety and as you realise you will soon be face to face with the enemy and you've got nothing, your anger fuelled confidence vanishes and your mind goes utterly blank. Finally, you step up to the lounging Russell, his casual, relaxed manner blasts away any last shreds of defiance in you and before you can speak, he compliments your hat. You thank him as he hands you a pre written signature and his security guard ushers you out of the way.

Feeling upset and impotent you go home and wallow in misery. Weeks go by and the black mood that has descended upon you doesn't shift, Mike gets worried and calls in a Doctor who explains that your symptoms are consistent with Post Traumatic Stress Disorder. One evening, in a final attempt to make the pain go away, you follow a YouTube instructional video and self-administer a lobotomy with a kebab skewer. It works, in a way.

You are dead.

## 25

As before the same cold, lisping recorded voice lists your options, you sign loudly from frustration and miss the first option, causing yourself to have to wait right until the end to hear them again.

Option one: If you are not a member and know nothing about who we are and what we do then press one (turn to 102)

Option two: To hear these options in Alpha Draconian press two (turn to 79)

Option three: If you are calling to receive your orders press three (turn to 94)

Get sick of listening to the options and decide to go to the address listed on the card (turn to 119)

## 26

Your stomach feels like a hot water bottle filled with boiling love, an overwhelming need to listen to Radio 1 and read celebrity magazines floods your brain. The chanting of the crowd grows feverish as you begin to dance and perform for them, Peter grins widely as you cavort like a marionette, so wrapped up in your impromptu performance you neglect to notice Mike being dragged away.

A teenage boys voice tears its passage through your throat and bursts from your mouth as you drop to your knees, ripping off your tee shirt.

If Russell Bland autographed your chest (turn to 64)

If all that adorns your moobs are sparse tufts of greying sweaty hair then (turn to 120)

## 27

Who needs possessions anyway, even on a temporary rental basis – as Brad Pitt said in Fight Club 'The things you own, end up owning you' and that was certainly true of Faisal the illegal immigrant slave your auntie Alice used to have. Still, even through all that nasty business she never once missed your weekly pocket money.

You successfully convince yourself once again that being free of material objects allows you to live a much richer life, not literally of course but spiritually. The realisation coincides with the overcast sky giving way to a bright sun, so you take a stroll down by the river feeling revitalised, the wind in your hair, both normal and facial.

Turn to 32.

## 28

You feel underqualified to advise on sexual reproduction but decide to plough on anyway, although you are unsure what Peter might already know so you start from the very beginning.

"Well." you say, gulping nervously "I got here because my mam and dad loved each other very much, albeit it briefly and they had sexual intercourse. Now sexual intercourse is when a man puts his tail in the womans secret and..." Peter, initially engrossed out sheer confusion now interrupts.

"I know how a human procreates you pathetic excuse for a carbon based life form, I am asking how you got in here, to our ceremony?" This does seem to you to be a more relevant question, so you tell him about the clues you followed that led you here.

Calming down Peter takes you aside and asks for your help with something in the underground lab. You initially think he means Labrador but you are led into a Laboratory, at the back of which are some rooms with one wall made of glass. Peter ask you to enter one of these rooms and then closes the door behind you.

Speaking through a receiver on the wall Peter explains that he was interested by your explanation of human reproduction and would like to witness it first-hand. A secret door opens and an attractive woman in her early twenties walks into your room, blinking in the bright light, naked and confused.

Your adventure ends here – or does it.

Bowm chikka bowm bowm!

## 29

The York streets look as beautiful as ever and you thank Xenu that you are able to eek out your existence in such a nice place. Through word of mouth you have heard tales of people living their full lives in places such as Middlesbrough or Wakefield and you despair that life can be so cruel.

Cutting through one of the many snickelways you find a timid, half-starved dog. The poor doggo stands about two feet tall, its fur is matted and patchy, you have limited knowledge of dog breeds but by the remnants of its golden coat you recognise it to be a Chocolate Labrador. The dog is curious and sniffs around you for food, quickly realising you have none and trots off away. Concerned for its wellbeing and also out of pure boredom, you skip after it.

Turn to 6.

## 30

The distance between you and Mike has grown (not just emotionally) and he is now near the front of the crowd which seems impossible for you to reach. Mike will surely know what this handwritten note means but the only way to get his attention it either wait and speak to him once you can reach him or shout his name right now like an uncouth yob.

Before you can really deliberate on the best option you find yourself already bleating out Mike's name, loudly and repeatedly. Even in that riotous din your voice soars clear above the rest and the crowd stops their clamour to turn and see where the high pitched keening is coming from. All at once the rooms eyes are on you, you fear you may have lost the element of surprise and figure it's probably best to get out of there so for one last time you shout 'Mike', only a little quieter to avoid further suspicion.

As the words leave your lips you watch helplessly as your friend is grabbed by two large, black suited men and his video equipment seized. He tries to fight but is brutally subdued (punched in the balls) and dragged away. Frantically, you pursue the men but are held back by many hands, a cloud of some sweet smelling spray engulfs your face and as you breathe in the vapour, you forget what was bothering you. Within a few minutes Peter Bones has resumed his speech and you take your place within the crowd.

Your journey ends here.


# 31

It isn't Sprite but it is equally as tasty, you grab the goblet with both hands and drain every last drop from its silvery innards. The liquid sloshes in your belly and fills you with a warm, contented feeling like after you've eaten Christmas Dinner but without the nausea. As you blink the room darkens but you notice all of the people within the hall are beginning to glow with a beautiful light. You turn to look at Mike, he is grey and seems distant (probably still in a bad mood) and seems to be shouting at you, although you can't hear his words. You run your hand down your sensuous form, prickling with a strange excitement.

If you picked up Mother Gaia's potion (turn to 118)

If you don't have the potion (turn to 26)


# 32

The river Ouse sparkles in the bright autumnal sunlight as you wade through the fallen leaves, a slight chill in the air hints at the coming of winter but after a few minutes walking you open your coat to let in the breeze and fend off the sweat dripping from your armpits. Cyclists pass by leisurely, mothers dawdle along with toddlers, office workers eat meals deals whilst cursing their choices in life, a skateboarder gets a conker trapped in his wheels and falls face first onto the concrete; it's a truly beautiful day to be alive.

You wipe some crud off a bench and perch to watch the world go by, absorbing the intoxicating atmosphere. In front of you amongst the leaves you see something gleam, bending down to inspect it you find a smartphone, on the protective case is a symbol: a triangle containing an eye. Wrestling your conscience you try and figure out the best thing to do.

Finders, keepers! You take the phone into town to see how much you can flog it for (turn to 78)

Noticing that the phone is unlocked you call the last number hoping it might give you some clue as to the owner (turn to 7)

Put the phone on the bench so that the rightful owner can come back later and find it (as long as no-one else has taken it in the meantime) (turn to 40)

## 33

Conrad fails to recognise your winking signal, so you ramp up the frequency until you just look totally mental. Eventually you work something into your eye, causing you to blink even more and furiously finger your socket to remove the foreign object. Conrad enquires if everything is ok with your eye and offers you his eye drops, never one to look a gift horse in the mouth you accept, lean back your head and drip some drops onto your troublesome peepers. Almost as soon as the liquid lands on the surface of your eyes the room around you seems to darken, you blink repeatedly as the colour seems to leach from the world.

In your peripheral vision you notice an incandescent, glowing object, almost too brilliant to look at. You squint your eyes slightly and are just able to make out the bright object, to your utter astonishment you realise it is Russell Bland! He sits on his chair like a golden god, enshrouded in an aura of white-hot fire, burning fiercely. His voice no longer sounds like fingernails dragged across a blackboard, it is now more beautiful than any other noise you have ever heard, it feels like warm honey is being spooned into your lugholes and even the content of his dialogue has changed from gratingly banal observations into sparklingly witty social commentary.

An urge to adore this divine creature overwhelms you, crossing your legs to inhibit ejaculation you:

Run out of the shop to get away (turn to 19)

Go to the staff toilets and wash your eyes (turn to 42)

Approach Russell Bland, boner protruding and drool dripping from your lower lip (turn to 61)

## 34

Your awkward acknowledgment of the old woman's existence causes her to grab your arm as you pass. You freeze in terror at the thought of contracting Hepatitis.

But your unsubstantiated prejudice turns to intrigue as the old woman comes closer "You are in danger Agravain Kestrel." she whispers in a youthful, feminine voice. The old woman lifts up the tattered rag concealing her face and reveals herself to be none other than The White Witch of the Woodland 'Mother Gaia'. Her grip tightens on your arm, as she slips a glass bottle containing a thick dark brown liquid into your jacket pocket. "They are every-where Kestrel and they are watching you. You have allies in this fight, take this potion, you will know when to use it. You must expose them or you will never go viral. They control everything. Everything. Including YouTube."

YOU NOW HAVE MOTHER GAIA'S POTION.

With that last warning Mother Gaia's grip on your arm releases and the blankets enshrouding her fall to the ground like Obi Wan's dressing gown. What did she mean? Who is watching you and when? You've masking taped your laptops built-in webcam, please god say that they can't can they see through that. And what possible use could this potion be, last time you had one of Mother Gaia's concoctions you vomited solidly for 24 hours and had a stonking boner that took days to shrivel.

An old flea ridden dog walks idly past and sniffs the blankets, he looks you in the eye and if you didn't know better you would swear he was flirting. The dog trots off down the street. Do you:

Follow the dog, convinced that he is some sort of spirit guide sent by Mother Gaia to aid you in your quest (turn tto 6)

Blush at the dogs advances and continue on into the Library (turn to 20)

**35**

You decline the offer but this doesn't go down too well with the crowd who begin chanting 'drink, drink, drink!' You are reminded of that fateful night in the woods when you were fourteen and a group of bigger boys pressured you into drinking White Lightning cider, hopefully this won't also end with you evacuating your bowels on the number 82 bus.

The two minions (that look a lot like Ant and Dec but can't possibly be) clutching your arms tighten their grip and urge you forward to the goblet. Ant (probably isn't) pinches your nose to make you open your mouth for air, Peter moves closer and is about to tip the liquid down your throat when Mike bursts out of his restraints, runs across and pushes the goblet out of Peter's hands, spilling the liquid onto the stone floor where it fizzes and bubbles. It must have been Sprite after all, what a waste!

Mike struggles with Ant and Dec (probably isn't them though), you have a moment in which to act:

If you have Mother Gaia's potion (turn to 116)

If you do not have the potion (turn to 15)

## 36

Shelf after shelf of high end Sci Fi novels present themselves to you as you keep walking to the teenage section to look for any new 'Goosebumps' or 'Point Horror' you may not have already read. Straining your neck at 90 degrees to read the titles on the books spines your hear someone say 'Pssst' and peer through the books to see a hunched figure wearing a hooded top, cargo shorts and a balaclava.

You look around to see who this mysterious figure is addressing and it gradually dawns on you, he might be speaking to you.

"Agravain Kestrel." He says in a rich, baritone voice "Stop looking all over the place like an idiot, I'm speaking to you!"

Slowly removing their balaclava this strange person reveals themselves to be your UFO obsessed, conspiracy riddled associate, Subject 14. He jigs nervously and glances around in a paranoid manner.

"I'm not sure how much you know so far." He says "But I have to be quick. They are watching. I think I'm next. It's the liquid. Don't drink the water, that's what they are using to control the sheeple."

It's not unusual to receive warnings like this from subject 14, most weeks you will get an email or letter from him panicking about an alien threat or government conspiracy, it's because of him you know that push bike saddles can give you AIDS. That said, you've never been contacted by him in person, he must be onto something really important to take such a risk. Instinctively you move closer, your proximity causes subject 14 to recoil back into the bookshelf, sending several books crashing down onto the wooden floor. All around you the library's inhabitants give you a loud collective 'Shhhh', you turn back to face Subject 14 but he has disappeared.

Gathering up the fallen books you spot a curious book called 'Brainwashed', a post it note stuck to the front cover reads 'Chapter 8'. You remove the post it note and decide to check this book out. You remove your library card from your ancient Animal wallet only to discover it has recently expired. Do you:

Go to the counter and renew your Library Card (turn to 2)

Slide the book into your jacket and walk out of the building whistling nonchalantly (turn to 47)

## 37

Digging deep you tense your under-used stomach muscles and clench your pelvic floor, determined to see this film through to the bitter end without accident. With the tip of your penis fizzing it's been dipped in sherbet you put in maximum effort and feel the wee begin to retract. As you shudder from exertion you hear a quiet popping noise and suddenly feel the urge to urinate disappear only to be replaced with excruciating abdominal pain. Sticking to your 'in for a penny, in for a pound' strategy you watch the remainder of the film before heading off to the toilet to assess the situation. Treating yourself to a sit down wee, you are upset to find your urine is actually bright red blood, you try a poo and find that although not all of it is blood, there is still more there than you'd like.

You walk home, slowly and call the doctor to make an appointment. Never one to make a fuss you answer 'No' when asked if it urgent and are given an appointment a fortnight later. Wondering how best not to aggravate your condition you cut out all fluids, yet you still keep on needing to go potty and each time it is about half a pint of blood.

Mike finds you in the back garden later that evening, at your funeral he describes how, when he found you, your body was all pale and white like the bit in ET when he is lying by the river.

You are dead.

## 38

You curse yourself for not actually going to the toilet whilst you were hiding and as the unusually tame and politically correct title credits roll you feel your bladder reaching its maximum limit. Desperate not to miss any of the film you cross your legs and try to focus on the plot but within thirty minutes you can no longer concentrate, your abdomen feels like the slightest nudge could set you off like a sprinkler system. What are you going to do?

Refuse to let yourself be pushed around by a bladder and hold it in right until the end of the film (turn to 37)

Relent and go for a nice, big wee wee (turn to 67)

## 39

Your eyes fix on Russell's and you feel caught in a tractor beam of unbridled carnal desire. Puckering your cracked lips your head suddenly lunges forward, catching him off guard and you plant a big wet smacker on Russell's own saintly gob. As your skin touches his a vivid image flashes through your mind: a human head, its skin being ripped off and revealing a green, scaly skull with bright yellow eyes. Shocked by the strange graphic imagery you recoil and are quickly scooped up by Russell's security team who take you somewhere to quietly beat you into a bloody unconscious heap.

You awake in a layby of the A64 battered, bruised and with less teeth than you remember. Unable to walk far you decide to stick out your broken thumb and hitchhike, much to your surprise being picked up within the first ten minutes. Also to your surprise your saviours are a group of born again Christian gypsies bound for Dover and despite your protests you are press ganged into helping tarmac roads in the South of France. As fate would have it, you find your calling in the relentless mixing, shovelling and smoothing of the tarry black substance and happily work solidly for the rest of your life, becoming an almost John Henry-esque figure in modern gypsy folklore.

Your adventure ends here.

## 40

You walk away, safe in the knowledge you are not a thief but also that you just passed up the opportunity of making enough money to buy a second hand Nintendo Switch. Oh well, it's not like you have the time to waste playing computer games anyway, you're a busy man!

A svelte jogger passes by, bound in skin tight Lycra and it reminds you that you are a bit fat. You compare their rippling torso to your own soft belly, poking at your flab with your chubby index finger.

"No time like the present!" you say out loud (to the surprise of a passing old woman) and set off jogging, convincing yourself that today is the day you finally turn your sad life around.

Your earflaps blowing in the wind, you ramp it up from a jog to a sprint, your body creaks and shunts like a gigantic, archaic locomotion suddenly forced in action after a thousand years. Sweat pours (literally pours) from your skin, pain shoots across your chest and sparkles form in front of your eyes, you feel faint. What do you do?

Decide this sensation must be what marathon runners call 'The Wall' and push on (turn to 90)

Stop now before you die (turn to 110)

# 41

As has become customary whilst sitting on the toilet you pull out you smart phone and start scrolling aimlessly through various social media sites, refreshing obsessively. Amongst the random garbage you see wedding photos of people you don't know, an advert for crowdfunding a new type of electric folding bike, a shitload of mediocre sunsets and argumentative comment threads on Brexit. Your head spins from both the eye-drops and the never-ending stream of semi-stimulating bullshit spewing from your phone screen so you put it away and sit back with your head against the wall, triggering the auto-flush that splashes cold water all over your bare buttocks. Drying off your cheeks you hear heavy footsteps enter the toilet and someone trying the cubicle door, you lean forward to ensure it is locked when the door is kicked wide open, hitting you flat in the face and knocking you so far backwards you once again trigger the auto-flush. Your head swims and as you fade into unconsciousness you watch helpless as your assailant takes down his pants, sits on the toilet and has a loud poo.

Turn to 56.

## 42

The toilet space is cramped and smelly, it reminds you of home. The plumbing whines and clatters in the walls as you run the cold tap, splashing water into your eyes. You struggle to comprehend what you have seen but luckily your mind has been conditioned to spot conspiracies where others are unable to do so, it is clear to you that something underhanded is going on.

You wonder what course of action would be most prudent.

Decide to kill two birds with one stone, sit on the porcelain throne and drop a deuce (turn to 41)

Slap yourself in the face, tell yourself to get a grip and get out on the streets to look for more evidence (turn to 19)

## 43

Patience was never your strong suit so rather than waiting to get home and writing a considered expose of the Chameleon club and their nefarious schemes, you tweet it. Almost immediately you receive an email telling you your Twitter account has been removed for posting inappropriate content, you try Facebook and find your account has been locked.

Feeling paranoid and just a little bit terrified you decide to go home and hide under your duvet until this blows over but as you begin to walk a man carrying a folded umbrella passes you and you feel a sharp prick in your thigh. The world becomes woozy, your vision leaves trails of colour in the air and you fall forward into the arms of a large man who bundles you into a van, slamming the doors and turning the world to black.

Turn to 56.

## 44

After a short while you come to a secluded car park near some woodland, Stephen Fry is rooting around nose first in a bin but as you approach him, his temperament suddenly changes. He growls and starts barking furiously, it occurs to you that you may have chosen the wrong name as his namesake would never be so aggressive, not towards a hard core QI fan like you anyway. Stephen Fry's snarling brings other dogs out from the treeline, one by one they slowly start to emerge, walking in your direction. 'Are these the QI elves Stephen?' you say nervously as fifteen to twenty medium sized dogs begin to converge on you but all you get in reply from Stephen Fry is another volley of loud barks. Before long the first dog reaches you, it snarls and snaps at your calf, as you turn around to try and shoo it away with your makeshift crutch a larger dog sinks its teeth into your forearm. The weight of the animal forces you onto your twisted ankle and you fall backwards to the ground, all at once the pack of hungry dogs are upon you in a frenzy of biting and tearing.

One street away a jogger hears you scream 'Why Stephen Fry, Why!??', later that night he tells his wife about it and they have a good laugh.


You are dead.

## 45

Reading the card again, 'The Chameleon Club' makes a lot more sense now you know the members can change their physical appearance – you had visions of Boy George for some reason. You've got to do something to expose this horrendous organisation before they realise you are onto them, with your high profile on social media your investigations must be on their radar, perhaps they are one of the 36 people who watched your most recent video last month.

There is no doubt that the best way to find people who will believe your story is to go on the internet, but is it worth trying to get some more conclusive evidence before posting it?

Grow some balls and go to the address on the card already (turn to 119)

Log onto the information super highway and plaster your expose, the phone number and address of The Chameleon Club all over social media (turn to 43)

## 46

For reasons you don't even understand yourself, you feebly cry out 'Help' in a high-pitched, ladies voice. The man moves towards your cell, the light from his tiny torch is blinding in this heavy darkness. The torch flicks off and you hear the scrape of metal and the sound of a key turning in the lock. With a rusty creak the door of your cell begins to open, what do you do?

Attack with all the fury and strength of a beta-male suffering from concussion (turn to 89)

Wait patiently like a good hostage to see what the nice man does (turn to 74)

# 47

The carefully concealed item burns in your jackets inside pocket like a red-hot nugget of pure shame. Society has driven you to this, you are not a devious criminal by nature, only nurture it would seem. The security guards beady eye follows you through the library as you walk ridiculously slowly to show you are not in a rush, the scrutiny of his gaze causes your face to go bright red and sweat to bead on your forehead, so you resemble a strawberry in the early morning dew.

Within a foot of the exit an arm suddenly blocks your way, it is the security guard you turn and meet his gaze. Gulping audibly, you ask

"Everything alright sir?" you ask, gulping audibly.

"You tell me" he responds glibly.

"Yes?" you reply, hoping it might be just that easy, but his facial expression quickly tells you it won't be.

"Can you please turn out your jacket pockets sir?" he says, so you do as you are told. Used tissues, bus tickets and an ancient, fluffy 'Chup-Chup' are piled onto a desk until you are finally forced to reveal your contraband. Busted!

The security guard whisks you into a back room and works you over thoroughly. During the beating you wonder who is guarding the library whilst he is in here kicking the stuffing out of you, but decide not to say anything. Within twenty minutes your burly captor begins to tire and lets you go free, hobbling away out of the back room and past the smug librarian you realise you still have the item in your coat pocket and hurry your pace. You got what you wanted in the end, 'he who laughs last, laughs longest' you think to yourself - they may just have to endure a lengthy physical assault first.

YOU HAVE THE BOOK 'BRAINWASHED'

Turn to page 122.

## 48

Years of pent up frustration borne from dealing with the worst members of the Great British public erupts from within Wulf Schmidt. Flipping the desk he rummages in his backpack withdrawing a vicious looking bowie knife which he holds to your throat. A tense hostage situation ensues, the police are called, Wulf communicates only in shrill screams demanding unrealistic things such as his own Yacht filled with lingerie models and at one point a skip full of custard doughnuts. After a nine hour stand-off armed police decide they have no choice but to storm the building, machine gunning down Wulf and unfortunately murdering you in the process. But look on the bright side, at least now you don't need to get a job.

You are dead and in several pieces.

## 49

You wait for the busker to finish his inferior version of someone else's song then approach him gingerly. As you get near the overpowering smell of alcohol makes you cough which alerts him to your presence and as he turns around to face you wearing a mask of pure anger you regret your decision.

"Wha tha fuck you starin' at pal?" he shouts in a Scottish accent so thick you could stand a spoon up in it. "Dya wan' a fuckin' shag pal eh? Is that it?" You shake your head from side to side to imply that sexual intercourse was not your intention but struggle to make any vocal response. In a vain attempt to indicate what you wanted you point at his money and manage to squeeze out the words 'Want money'. This course of action sends the inebriated minstrel into a frothing rage and he kisses you heavily on the nose with his forehead causing you to stumble backwards and crack your skull on the pavement.

As you bleed out your murderer plays a truly awful version of 'Weather with you' by Crowded House.

You are dead.

## 50

You catch Mike's attention in the crowd and signal that you are going to chat with Peter Bones, he waves frantically and shakes his head to let you know he agrees with your plan. Pushing through the transfixed mob you emerge behind Peter as he talking. So you don't frighten him when he turns around you loudly yell out his name.

Peter jumps and stops mid-sentence and he turns his gaze towards you the crowd also seem to notice you, very politely falling completely silent so you can have a civil conversation without shouting.

"Who are you?" Peter demands.

"I'm Agravain Kestrel, professional paranormal enthusiast." you say in return, adding redundantly "You look tall on the telly but even taller in real life." With a click of his fingers Peter beckons over two of his minions who grasp your arms, Peter looms over you and once again speaks.

"How did you get here!" he says. It's a big question, how do you reply?

Have 'the talk' with Peter about sexual reproduction in humans (turn to 28)

Take a very existential slant on Peters question, ramble for two minutes about reincarnation until you are confused and then tail off into an awkward silence (turn to 105)

Ignore his question and tell him you are looking for the Illuminati (turn to 59)

## 51

Curling up you pull the covers over your squashy form in a physical manifestation of the psychological barrier it represents.

Eager to re-enter your previous dream you think back to when you were a teenager and you got a book called 'How to Astral Project' from the library. Many a night you tried to induce lucid dreaming through various meditative breathing techniques but never truly managed it, the closest you got was waking up unable to move or speak for a full five minutes which was apparently a good sign but scared you so much you never tried again. However, this morning without much effort you achieve your teenage goal of being awake within a dream, remembering your training you know the key is to move through the astral plane using vibrations, but you can't find a way to easily vibrate so you walk, soon finding yourself at your childhood home. Behind you a thin golden thread trails and drifts on the air like spider silk, you recognise this as your 'astral cord' linking you back to your sleeping body in the real world. The door opens with ease and you walk into the house, immediately met with the sights, sounds and smells of your youth. A greyish blue pall of acrid cigarette smoke hangs in the air, from within the living room your mother's familiar hacking cough can be heard.

"Good job fresh air's free! Put wood int' hole you lumbering idiot, you're letting a draught in!" she shouts through a throatful of thick phlegm. At the sound of your mothers braying voice you instinctively turn around and close the front door, chopping your astral cord clean in half.

Later that day Mike enters your room and finds your cold, blue body curled up in bed, both him and the coroner cannot explain why your clothes and sheets smell of cigarette smoke but dismiss it as unimportant and your death is officially recorded as 'a probable overdose of jaffa cakes'.

You are dead.

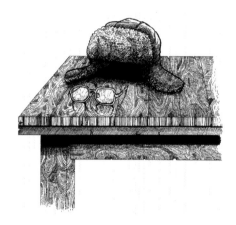

## 52

The door at the back of the cinema opens suddenly and for a brief panic stricken moment you think that you've been rumbled. It quickly becomes apparent that it isn't the cinema security looking to chuck you out but just a couple of annoying female, teenage latecomers who giggle their way down the aisle and plonk themselves directly behind you.

Within minutes the irksome pair have begun talking, nudging the back of your chair and unwrapping sweets maliciously. You give them the classic 90-degree head turn to display your annoyance but it only prompts them to laugh more, all you have left in your arsenal is a loud tut but that could cause everything to 'kick off big style'. The situation escalates as you feel a piece of popcorn hit the back of your head, followed by another and another, in a show of defiance you pick one of the pieces off your shoulder and eat it, at which point one of the girls coughs the word 'scratter'. Your blood begins to boil at their lack of respect, it's disgusting how people abuse the cinema, if you had actually paid for your ticket you'd ask for your money back. You decide to try and persevere with the film and turn the other cheek, then the kicking starts.

If you decide to refrain from confrontation because of your natural cowardice (turn to 62)

If you decide to hide your cowardice by pretending to take the moral high ground (turn to 62)

## 53

You are used to stumbling upon things: stairs, kerbs and so on but this takes the biscuit. Wait until you tell the lads on the conspiracy-uk forums about this one, they'll have to re-consider your bid to become a moderator now, especially if they let Wayne be one just for taking some shit blurry UFO photos. It is imperative that you expose this wicked plot before a real field agent is deployed and even though a small part of you has always wondered what it is like to be a woman, the thought of altering your appearance sounds scary and you are a coward first and foremost.

If you have the business card from 'The Lizard' DVD case (turn to 45)

If you have no idea who this organisation/club giving you orders actually is (turn to 101)

## 54

Luckily for you the average age of the cinema staff is twenty-three and even that has been thrown off wildly by one male employee who looks like he is in his mid-forties, needless to say they aren't too tight on security and you manage to slip past by hiding behind various oversized cardboard cut-outs. Moving semi silently from your last hiding place you make a break for the velvet rope barrier planning to leap it and land into a forward roll, that doesn't quite happen. Catching your shoe on the rope you turn upside down in the air and land on the top of your head, all of the teenage staff stare at you for a tense five seconds then get back to 'work', eager to avoid having to fill in the accident report log. As you pick yourself up off the ground the mid-forty something employee approaches you, he leans in, introduces himself as Max and explains that he knows what you are up to. Before you can construct an elaborate lie, Max explains that he is not technically employed by the cinema. Although he spends every day there and works a 60 hour week, he does not get paid, it is all part of a clever plan to watch films without paying. You notice a flaw in his logic and ask him why he doesn't just get a job there and earn enough money to be able to pay to watch the films but he has clearly thought things through explaining that 'This way the films are free'. He gives you an ill-fitting airtex top and you join him on his devious mission for the next thirty four years of your life until the cinema shuts. Throughout those years Max saves you from choking on popcorn no less than eleven times.

Your adventure ends here.

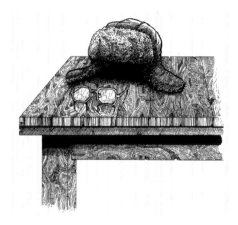

## 55

Whilst waiting for the computer to boot up you have a quick shower, make some breakfast and watch the last fifteen minutes of Frasier. You cancel the twenty or so pop ups and warning messages from your desktop then open Internet Explorer, another ten minutes pass until finally the screen unfreezes and you are free to surf the world wide web. Somewhat inevitably you wind your way to the usual electronic auction site that has been the location of so many unnecessary purchases over the years. Fully aware that you have absolutely no money you type in 'Genuine Cryptid Artefacts' and are presented with several pages of extremely dubious and outrageously expensive objects. There are plaster casts of Bigfoot tracks, Nessie Ambergris, a Chupacabra paw, Jackalope antlers, you name it, it's on there. You finally decide to pay up front to pre-order a Unicorn horn for when one becomes available, you add it to the basket and cross your fingers as you process it through on your credit card, the statement of which you haven't read in 18 months. Surprisingly the payment goes through but as a result your identity is stolen many thousands of miles away by an individual in China. You receive many notifications via email and text about suspicious activity on your accounts and after many days you realise what has happened but decide to let them keep your identity (you weren't using it all that much anyway) and think nothing more about it. Within another month the situation has escalated dramatically, your identity has been used in several cases of international espionage causing you to be extradited to China where you are incarcerated indefinitely. After much confusion and pleading you are given one phone call which you use to contact Mike to give him your new address so he can forward on the Unicorn horn when it arrives. You spend the next forty years of your life here until you succumb to avian flu.

You are dead.

## 56

Your eyes flicker open but the world remains inky black, your head feels as bad as the time Mike bet you that you couldn't drink two beers. As you try and stand, your flaccid legs wobble back and forth like a macabre imitation of Elvis Presley dancing, then give way sending you crashing to the damp, cold stone floor.

Lying there on the ground your mind wanders and begins to taunt you with images of delicious food and drink. You inwardly decide that at this moment in time you would happily take another man's life for a drink of Tizer. Obviously it would have to be a bad man like Hitler, Chairman Meow or whoever it was that drew an incredibly detailed 3D penis on Mike's front door last week - although to be fair, the guy had talent. When your first saw it you actually thought it was an erotic doorknocker.

Anyway, you come out of your reverie desperately thirsty and in-stinctively begin lapping at a puddle with your tongue, the liquid has a strange flavour, it's too grainy to be water but it is quench-ing. In the distance you hear anguished shrieks and the occasional moan of despair. You manage to feel your way across the floor and around the walls to a locked doorway but realise with dread that you are in some sort of dank prison cell with extremely limited facilities. Having spent many a childhood summer in Pontins you are no stranger to these conditions, you feel a nostalgic glow, then pass out again.

You are awoken by the noise of heavy footsteps outside your cell, by the light of a dim torch you see these footsteps come from a pair of feet that are attached to a man who appears to be searching the cells. Do you:

Play dead by rolling onto your back and sticking your arms and feet into the air (turn to 84)

Hold back the imminent tears and try and get the attention of the man (turn to 46)

# 57

You spring out of bed with all of the grace and energy of a preg-nant heifer, pull on some 'clean' underpants and dowse your torso with Lynx Africa as a quick but frankly inadequate alternative to a shower. Dressing in your favourite outfit (brown cords, Spock tee shirt) you stroll past your housemate Mike's bedroom, the smell of intestinal gas wafts through the open door and across your sleepy eyes making them water.

Downstairs you resurrect the living room by tidying away Mike's empty beer cans, opening the curtains and giving the sofa a heavy Febreezing. The clock reads 4:47pm as always, you curse the high price of batteries and check your watch for the real time, 9:55am. If you are going to get to the Job centre in time you'd better hurry, do you:

Pull on your battered Hi-Tecs and pound the pavement (turn to 11)

Raid the piggy bank for some bus fare (turn to 97)

Admit defeat, collapse in a depressed heap and willingly hurtle headfirst into the refuge of the damned that is daytime TV (turn to 70)

## 58

Reluctantly you hand over your five pound note, the Librarian becomes a blur of administration and within a couple of minutes you are furnished with a new shiny Library card. You shakily sign the back then and with adrenaline pumping through your veins you pop your book on the counter ready to be stamped.

YOU NOW HAVE THE BOOK 'BRAINWASHED'.

Eager to see what the Post-It note was referring to you immediately find a quiet spot in the corner of the Library, sitting down behind a large shelf. You look at the cover of the book and then start to flick through the pages to chapter 8 but before you can reach it you feel an almighty blow to the top of your head and the world fades into black.

Turn to 56.

## 59

Peter looks at you dumbfounded.

"You are looking for the Illuminati? Who the hell do you think we are?" You shrug and look at Mike. "No idea?" you reply "What do you reckon Mike?" Mike glances around desperately and tries to run but with another click of Peter's fingers he is detained alongside you. Mike gives you a hacky look, he can be so moody!

Circling you both Peter begins addressing the crowd again.

"He wants to find The Illuminati!" he shouts and lets out a huge laugh, the audience spontaneously jeer and clap "Oh but Kestrel." he says "The only way to truly see what you are after is to join us!" He produces an ornate goblet brimming with clear, bubbly liquid and offers it to you. You look at Mike, he shakes his head. What do you do:

Well you didn't come this far to NOT find out who the Illuminati are, besides, that looks like Sprite in the goblet so you greedily guzzle down the liquid (turn to 31)

Tell Peter that's precisely what Sky said to you and you ended up in a 24 month contract, never again (turn to 35)

## 60

As soon as you turn on the app you notice several different 'Jaba-guys' near your location, you catch a few crappy ones and mince them to feed your other imprisoned 'Jabaguys'. Within minutes you are spoiled for choice as three prime 'Jabaguys' appear on screen, none of which you have previously detained against their will:

If you want to catch a gigantic pink cloud with a bow on its head lurking by the river (turn to 13)

If you want to catch an electrical, hovering sphere with a terrifying human face near the Shambles (turn to 21)

If you want to catch a one-eyed, karate obsessed monstrosity in Argos (turn to 10)

# 61

You bulldoze through the queue, ignoring the furious objections until you are standing opposite Russell, his raw sexuality hits you like a Tsunami and for a brief, intimate moment his gaze meets your own.

"Felicitations my keen admirer." he says in a faux cockney accent, gesticulating like he is in a pantomime "You're an eager beaver aren't you!" His security guards flank you and grab your arms, meaning to drag you away and dispose of you but Russell holds up his hand and shouts "Halt and be still my cheeky protectors, unhand this enfusiastic yoof." He waves away his massive body-guards and then once again fixes you with his dazzling eyes "Well, park your derriere up on this tableau." he says "And I shall furnish you wiv my 'umble moniker." He pulls out a marker pen and leans in, you now understand that he means to reward your 'pushing in' with an autograph, what do you do?

Get caught up in the moment and feeling confused by Russell's proximity, kiss him on the lips as he leans over to give you his autograph (turn to 39)

Pull off your Tee Shirt so Russell can scrawl his meticulously practiced signature across your soft pectoral muscles (turn to 77)

## 62

You do nothing as the taunting continues throughout the entire film, your aggressors spurred on by your apparent inaction as you shrink inside yourself, filled with self-loathing. As the credits roll you wait for the cinema to clear out, only then once you are sure you will not bump into your teenage tormenters do you allow yourself to leave.

Exiting the cinema you notice that the busker is still caterwauling his way through his limited catalogue, but he is doing it with passion and conviction that it raises your spirits. Regardless of the guys talent he has more money in his guitar case than you've seen for several months. A crazy idea flashes across your brain, perhaps you could get in on this cash cow? Do you:

Wait for the busker to stop and propose that you do a couple of duets for a slice of his cash rich pie (turn to 49)

Watch the busker for a few moments, then as your enthusiasm is overpowered by doubt, go kick some leaves along the side of the river (turn to 32)

# 63

You shout and scream until your throat feels raw and eventually you see the light of a torch shining down a distant corridor.

A deep, gruff voice shouts "Shut up you whining little twat!".

Finally, you have someone's attention so you shout loud and whinier, prompting another gravelly response, this time with a threat of impending violence if your hooting doesn't cease immediately. Not to be deterred by idle threats (you are used to working with Mike) you let out the most pathetic 'Help' the world has ever known and are pleased to see it brings your unknown correspondent into the room. A huge man stands in the centre of the room, breathing hard and shining the torch in your face.

"Didn't I tell you to stop shouting? I've got a F@"#ing migraine" he shouts then unlocks you cell door.

At last, you think, glorious freedom! You rush out to hug your saviour but far from returning your warm embrace he clutches your throat with his jumbo sized hand and lifts you into the air. Your feet dangle like a newborn baby's as the gigantic man's grip tightens around your neck causing a crunchy noise. In a final attempt to struggle free you weakly hit the man on the arm which instantly enrages him further, he raises you up, headfirst into the stone ceiling again and again, smashing your skull like a chocolate Easter egg.


You are dead.

## 64

The moment your torso is unveiled a strange gasp comes up from the crowd and everyone, including Peter, falls prostrate in reverence to the writing on your chest. Snapping momentarily out of your fugue state, you glance down at your pale body to see Russell Bland's autograph shining white hot like an etching made of pure sunlight. Peter approaches you and places his hand on your shoulder and turns to the crowd.

"He has been chosen." he says in a gentle but clear voice "Behold the next big thing! All hail Kestrel!" The acolytes echo their masters cry until the whole room are singing your praise in one autotuned voice.

The weeks following are a blur, you do The One Show, Sunday Brunch, Graham Norton, your fame growing wildly with every passing day. Kestrel Investigates trends on twitter causing YouTube to crash for the first time since it's invention, you are seen with the Beckhams in a fashionable nightspot, you feature as a guest vocalist on the new George Ezra single, everyone wants a piece of Kestrel.

After a while the furore dies down and you go back to making Kestrel Investigates, but it's not the same without Mike, you can't even remember what happened to him. In an attempt to remain relevant, you sign up for Strictly and get to the last four, the tabloids print an expose on an illicit affair you share with Tess Daley but no-one really cares. Finally you hit rock bottom and appear on Celebrity Big Brother, you breakdown and cry on national television but by this point only a handful of people are watching and even those are merely glancing over their mobile phones whilst they prowl Twitter like a murderer in a red light district. You go into rehab after developing an addiction to silverskin pickled onions and balloon in weight. Your remaining days are spent as a side show at conventions being pestered by obsessive fans for photographs, praying for death.

Well done, you found the fame you always wanted, was it worth it?!

## 65

Time seems to halt as you sit in the pitch black of your cell, the dark stasis closes in around you making you feel claustrophobic. You search your coat for your mobile phone but it has been taken by your abductors, you curse yourself for not deleting your internet browser search history more regularly and cross your fingers that they don't figure out your passcode.

For what seems like hours you sit alone and wonder what you could have done to end up here. What if this isn't a simple case of mistaken identity? Through your investigations you have made some enemies, that's all part and parcel of being a serious journalist but you can't imagine anyone going to such lengths just to detain you. After wracking your brain you decide this can be linked to only two things: the time you went through the self-service at Morrisons and neglected to pay for the carrier bag or when you burnt down a historic church by exploring using a flaming torch. In this situation it's all just speculation. The waiting is starting to really hack you off. Do you:

Keep waiting like a good boy (turn to 72)

Shout out apologies for the bag and the church in the hope that your honesty gets you released (turn to 63)

## 66

Why anyone would want to infiltrate the Yorkshire Country-woman's Association other than to find the recipe of their delicious cakes is beyond you! Anyway, what would Nanna Kestrel say if you had anything to do with the Yorkshire Countrywoman's Association? Well nothing, because she is dead, but if she wasn't, she'd be really miffed as a lifelong member of the East Yorkshire Woman's Institute – in fact she would probably 'kick off' as she so frequently did.

You press the button to go back to the beginning of the options.

Turn to 25.

## 67

Struggling to find your seat you decide to check your ticket, soon locating the right aisle and chair. Sitting down it suddenly occurs to you that you are in a completely different location than before, you recheck your ticket and see that it is for 'Nuts', then remember that you snuck into this film and therefore don't have a ticket. Relaxing back into the film you watch Bond take off his bra and strangle a worthless henchman, quipping as he drops the dead body 'Breast have a lie down'.

Stretching out, your hand feels something in the cupholder, it is a bag of sweets! Get in! Glancing around to make sure nobody is watching, you sneakily grab them and stick them in your pocket then carry on watching Bond do his/her thing.

YOU FOUND A BAG OF SWEETS!

Turn to 52.

## 68

Using the frankly inadequate LED torch Mike has brought on his car keys you both work your way down a corridor until you come to a T junction. Mike comments that this is the sort of lazily written situations one would find in those choose your own adventure books he read as a child but shrug off his opinion as unnecessarily negative. Nonetheless, you need to make yet another decision based on pure luck. Both tunnels seem identical apart from the sounds emanating forth, from the left you hear raucous cheering, to the right you hear laughter. Which way do you choose:

Go left towards the cheering (turn to 109)

Go right towards the laughter (turn to 3)

## 69

The first car you see borders yellow and orange, you know the colour would be classed as 'Sunburst Yellow' by the dealership yet it's quite clearly a light orange. Stumped by this conundrum you shift to green just in time to notice the bus pulling away from your intended stop. You press the button but the driver continues driving until the next stop and you are forced to walk back to the job centre.

Turn to 9.

## 70

You watch program after program about homes, antiques and

inheritance hunters, sliding slowly down on the sofa. Morning passes into midday, midday into afternoon, afternoon into evening. Through the living room window you see real people coming home from work after meaningful, productive days contributing to society. A single tear strolls down your cheek into your scruffy stubble and as you gaze slack-jawed at Richard Osman quipping to the audience on Pointless, you realise you have suffered a fate worse than death, you have spent another full day watching daytime television.

Your adventure ends here.

# 71

"Come on Mike, hurry up!" you whine. Mike tells you to shut up and turns on the camera, pointing it at Peter Bones as he begins once again to walk around the circle, talking loudly to the baying crowd.

"Let us see if the next act is worthy!" he shouts and from a small gap in the crowd emerges a nervous looking middle-aged woman. The jeers grows steadily quieter as Peter gestures for silence but before the next victim can perform Peter seems to glance in Mike's direction, you can see from your position that the lens of the camera is glinting. Peter clicks his fingers and as you turn around to flee a heavy blow to your head turns out the lights.

You are dead.

## 72

In an attempt to entertain yourself you recite the entirety of the 1988 fantasy film 'Willow' out loud, figuring that if you can do this continuously, without sleeping, you can count the passage of time in 126 minute increments. By the fourth recital you start to enact the action scenes and during an animated fight scene in which you are throwing magic acorns at a troll in Tir Asleen you rap your knuckles on a stone wall, taking off a thick layer of skin from every digit. Clutching your bloody hand you sink back into a depressed funk and allow the passage of time to continue onwards unbridled.

Several hours probably pass, you are forced to urinate in the corner of your cell but draw the line at doing a number two. You can't hold it in forever though.

Try and get someone's attention by shouting 'brown alert' through the bars on your door (turn to 63)

Keep waiting whilst lying on the floor with your legs up the wall hoping gravity will encourage the encroaching faeces to backtrack (turn to 82)

## 73

Remembering the 'Post It' note Subject 14 had left on the front cover of 'Brainwashed' you quickly flick to Chapter 8 and read the title 'Illuminati'. You have no idea what that word means but in the margin of the book is a badly handwritten note 'I have proof now, look in their eyes! It's mass hypnosis to dumb down mainstream culture! Do not use the eyedrops or you'll become a Lizardman'. You duck down to the ground to stop the screaming crowd from jostling you, Mike fails to see and continues to the front of the audience.

Peter Bones continues his coincidentally well timed expositional speech as you flick through the book for more writing but find none.

"And now loyal subjects we have developed a way to move beyond eyedrops." Booms the tall entrepreneur. "We have created a new version of compound X-Factor that we will release into the UK water supply at midnight tonight. Soon everyone in this questionably great country will share our vision... because the compound changes people's eyes to lizard eyes and that makes them see banal pedestrians as extraordinarily talented entertainers. You've seen our trials with pop musicians over the years and more recently judge based talent competitions. Yeah? Does everyone understand the evil plan? Well, point made."

You struggle to comprehend the details of Peter Bones' nefarious scheme, but you have learnt to use your intuition and decide these guys must be able to help you find the Illuminati, if only you understood what the handwritten message in the book meant!

Enter the circle and ask Peter Bones where you can find the Illuminati (turn to 50)

Speak to Mike about the hidden message in the book (turn to 30)

## 74

The man opens the door wide, enters the cell and towers over your prone body, the torchlight totally blotting out his shape. You lie there expecting him to deliver a killing blow but instead he squats down, puts his hand on your shoulder.

"Kes, it's Mike." he says softly.

You burst into floods of tears, incomprehensible babble spews from your distorted gurgling mouth as Mike helps you up onto your feet. He reveals that you are deep below York Minster and that he was contacted by an anonymous source that told him you were being held here. For the next five minutes you tell him that you love him and basically make an embarrassing mess of yourself until finally you snap out of it. Mike suggests you get out of there immediately and continue to investigate above ground.

If you have no mind of your own and want to follow Mike blindly

(turn to 104)

If you have a death-wish and want to extend that to Mike by continuing to search underground (turn to 68)

## 75

"Your assignment is accepted – stay on the call to hear more" a deep, otherworldly voice announces. As directed you listen intently as the details of 'the plan' are spilled by that same, unfeeling, inhuman voice.

"Well met agent, this will not be an easy mission, do not be fooled by their friendly appearance – this organisation has foiled several of our plots previously, the Yorkshire Countrywoman's Association are not to be trifled with. You are to alter your form to that of Mrs Connie Wretton, 71 year old resident of Fangfoss who is currently under surveillance. We will arrange for her to be removed so that you can take her place when ready. We will send you further details in an encoded email, check your junk within five minutes from the end of this call. Once in position we will fully reveal the nature of your assignment – but make no mistake, this mission is kill or be killed".

Turn to 53.

## 76

A loud, gutteral, snarling voice barks out a harsh, jarring language – potentially German. The incomprehensible speech carries on for ages and then abruptly stops, so far all of these have pretty muh boiled down to two options so you decide to press either one or two.

Option one (turn to 22)

Option two (turn to 106)

## 77

Russell unclicks the lid of marker pen and touches the nib against your skin, moving it expertly across the pale, goose-bumped surface to create his contrived and ostentatious hallmark. As the pen whips and loops around, your eyes flicker and you suddenly become hugely aware of where you are and what is happening. Embarrassment rises up inside you like steam causing your face to go crimson, your eyes sting and you realise your vision has been impaired. As Russell finishes his handywork with a harshly jabbed full stop, you shamefully roll down your Tee Shirt and walk, head down in shame, into the staff toilets to clean your balls (eyeballs).

Turn to 42.

## 78

It used to be that York was famous for having a pub for each day of the year, truly that could be said about phone shops these days. The choice is staggering but you have experience of selling your possessions regularly so you know where to go for the best deals. Down a back street you go to 'Greg's phone and spinal repairs' a little known boutique that specialises in repairing smart phones and chiropractic services.

Thankfully the shop is open, which is often not the case (you try to support these independent retailers but they don't help themselves sometimes) so you wander in and show Greg your phone. He turns it over in his hands, raising his eyebrows and makes you an offer of 50 quid and quick spinal manipulation as long as you take it right now. You accept, Greg closes the shop, loses the blinds and ushers you into the back room where you hop straight up onto his massage table like an eager dog at the vets.

Greg enquires if you have any problem areas and you mention that your neck has been very stiff ever since you last came in and he manipulated your neck. He nods and tells you that in order to loosen it he has to 'crack' your neck (seems harmless) so he grabs you with one hand under your jaw and another at the back of your head.

"I'm sorry Kes, you shouldn't have messed with things you don't understand." Greg says through tear filled eyes, then like a villain in an action movie, he violently twists. Your neck certainly does crack and you feel all the pain go from your body, along with any feeling you ever had below the shoulders. Greg looks over you holding the phone and as your start lose your vision, tears rolls down his tattooed cheeks. Greg is convicted of murder later that month when a woman in the local butcher finds part of a lens from your glasses in a Steak pie.


You are dead – and oh so tasty!

# 79

God knows why but you decide you'd like to hear the options in a language you've never heard of and sure enough, once you've pressed option two the voice on the other end of the phone changes. Instead of a cold, hard English voice there is a high pitched hissing noise that you don't understand – the only language you did at school was French and you got an E in that, although you pride yourself in being able to 'I am a tortoise' in German (Ich bin eine Schildkröte).

The weird voice speaks in two distinct blocks so you assume that it has once again given you two options, obviously you have no idea what these are but you have made it this far so you trust your instincts.

Option one – a long rasping hiss followed by several short hacking cough noises and what sounds like a meow (turn to 81)

Option two – a wheezing, whispering hiss punctuated by a snorting noise (turn to 76)

## 80

You run wildly through the labyrinthine streets of York, eyes wide in panic and thick clear snot trailing from your nose like uncooked egg white. Severe chest cramps force you to stop and as you stand, bent double, swallowing huge gulps of air you realise you are outside York Library. Ahh the library, warm, dry and free, many a relaxing day you have spent in there out of Mike's way, sitting quietly.

Next to the doorway in a crumpled heap of blankets sits an old homeless woman, her face obscured by rags as she gestures a cardboard cup towards you, pleading for charity. In reality, she is almost certainly in a better financial position than you are. Do you:

Pat your empty pockets, mumble a weak apology and head towards the library doorway (turn to 34)

Totally ignore her like a heartless bastard and walk straight in (turn to 30)

## 81

You press the 'one' button and hear a bleep immediately followed by more strange speech. As before there are two seperate pieces of incomprehesible noise, but you persevere anyway and choose one.

Option one – two anguished yelps, a whistle and some sort of cross between humming and shouting (turn to 88)

Option two – a gentle sighing noise (turn to 5)

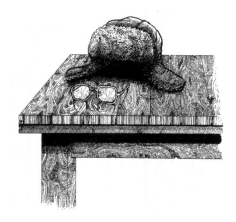

## 82

You shit your pants. In the darkness you cannot see precisely where the offending poo is but you get a general sense from the smell, heat and weight. You remove your clothes quickly and bundle your underpants up, flinging them through the bars of your door. Forced to go commando you pull you trousers back, dragging them through your cold urine that has clearly run from the corner and pooled itself near your feet.

Your discomfort now dealt with your mind once again returns to your predicament, you try to stay optimistic by thinking of a jolly song but all that comes to mind is the irritatingly catchy smash hit 'The Birdy Song'. You play this song in your head on repeat, each time it seems to get louder and just a little faster. The cell begins to feel very warm as the melody cycles in your brain, again and again and again and again. You take off your shoes to cool yourself down and immediately stand in your own piss again. A scream builds in your throat.

Swallow that scream, wring out your socks and keep waiting (turn to 93)

Scream the F word very loudly (turn to 63)

## 83

Wulf lets out a deep growl as you slide your sweaty, odorous form onto the chair opposite him. Your pulse thumps the inside of your skull like a speed metal, double kick drum. Wulf shuffles some papers then fixes you with an exasperated gaze.

In a weary voice Wulf says "Good morning Agravain, how's the job search going?"

Glancing around frantically for inspiration you try to think of a realistic sounding story to satisfy the Wulf's hunger and with a dry mouth you start to speak, not knowing exactly what is about to spew forth.

What do you tell Wulf?

That his name makes him sound like a Gladiator and inform him that as a lazy, unskilled British citizen it is your right to receive a small fortnightly allowance paid for by the taxes of others so gimme gimme gimme! (turn to 48)

That your job search is going well, no employment so far, but you don't feel the need to bog him down in the minute details of your fruitless search. You are a busy man, places to go (home), people to see (Mike), so if you can just sign the form and get going that would be swell (turn to 12)

Since your last encounter you have tirelessly scoured the local papers, internet and even gone door to door in local businesses but have so far been found lacking in both experience and ability, the endless unemployment is sapping your feeling of self-worth and most days you wander the streets like a phantom existing in the same plain as the living but unseen and unwelcome. Then begin crying (turn to 4)

# 84

As the unknown person creeps from cell to cell you imitate a corpse, pulling a ragged blanket over your body and turning your face to the wall, you have a tendency to giggle in stressful situations and that would give the game away. Through your closed eyelids you sense a torch being shined over you, then you hear the prowling footsteps head off in another direction.

Having safely hidden from the intruder you lie down on the wooden bench and for the first time have a good think about your situation. Luckily you are experienced in dealing with enforced isolation having been trapped in a Debenhams changing room over night when you were in your early twenties. Unfortunately this time you don't have a multipack of pickled onion corn snacks to keep your spirits buoyant so in an attempt to rid yourself of the intense headache you are suffering with you go back to sleep.

An unknown amount of time passes and you awake once more in total darkness. Thankfully your head feels slightly better but you are starting to feel hungry and have no idea where you are or why. The uncertainty plays on your mind. Do you:

Keep waiting patiently for someone to come along so you can

explain that they have made a mistake, be released and hopefully receive some sort of financial compensation/treat (turn to 65)

Repeatedly shout out that you are hungry in the whiniest voice you can muster to make it impossible to ignore (turn to 63)

## 85

You browse the DVDs and ruminate that you never see anyone else looking at these, in many ways these shelves are your very own Netflix. The Horror/Sci Fi section throws up the usual guff, the only ones you haven't seen several times before are two nineties Keanu Reeves films 'Chain Reaction' and 'Johnny Mnemonic' but you draw the line at these considering your time too valuable to waste on them, instead you stray into the crime section picking up the 1972 film 'The Lizard', a movie you have watched eight times previously.

As you pick up the DVD case you feel the something inside fall loose, so you open it to find a small golden card with the words 'The Chameleon Club' embossed on the front.

You decide to pop the DVD back on the shelf and investigate this curious card a little more

Turn to 114.

## 86

Mother Gaia told you the right moment would present itself and with Peter rapidly approaching you turn your back and unscrew the lid, then down the foul tasting potion in one. The thick, syrupy liquid oozes down your throat, causing a warming, almost burning sensation. Peter grabs you from behind and restrains your hands and starts to lead you away from the ceremonial chamber, but within about a minute from ingesting the potion you start to feel funny, and not in a good way. Deep in the pit of your stomach you feel a queasy pain which causes you to collapse in a heap. Jets of excrement splash from your backside and yellow vomit belches from your mouth as you writhe around on the stone floor, covered in both. Peter and the guards stand back as you spin around like a human Catherine wheel, continually emptying your contents until, as seem to be usual with Mother Gaia's potions you feel a stirring in your loins and an unwanted but unstoppable erection raises its ugly head.

People disperse from disgust, Peter, Ant and Dec all leave shaking their heads and muttering. Mike takes you home and after several weeks your member returns back to its usual inoffensive, diminutive state. Mike 'leaks' the video onto YouTube and it goes viral after being 'Tweeted' by J.K.Rowling.


Your adventure ends here.

## 87

You walk a couple of miles before reaching Waitrose. As you approach the door you hear the most sublime piano music emanating from the entrance. The automatic doors open gently with a pleasing swishing sound and a warm curtain of air greets your skin as you gaze into the shop. All around you are smiling faces as you float along the beautifully arranged aisles, a faint perfume of bergamot lingers in the air like an angel's body odour. An attractive woman smiles at you as she pushes her perfectly maintained trolley past you and for the first time in your life you have a feeling of acceptance. Using your five pound note you buy some caramelised almonds, the type your grandmother always used to buy. Gaily skipping through the carpark on a wave of ecstasy, a rogue almond lodges itself in your windpipe, obscured by an ocean of Range Rovers nobody notices your final struggle as you choke to death on the cold hard tarmac.

Your are dead.

## 88

Suddenly the voice changes back to English and says 'welcome agent, you will receive your orders promptly, please make sure you are using a secure line.

Turn to 75.

## 89

Slowly the man opens the cell door and steps inside pointing the tiny light towards you. Keeping your face slightly hidden you wait until the person gets nearer, then you attack! First knocking the light out of his hand and across the cell floor then secondly lashing out wildly with your spinning arms and kicking feet, catching him once across the chest and once squarely in the balls. Seeing your foe drop to the ground in pain you make a break for the open doorway but are tripped, cracking your cheek on the stone doorframe. As you roll over your assailant leaps onto you and you roll about entangled, viciously gouging, biting, punching, elbowing and even pulling hair. Ultimately you are outmatched and your opponent slams your forehead into the ground, crushing your skull and causing terminal damage. Backing off and breathing hard he picks up his torch and shines it down on your dying and convulsing body then suddenly lets out an anguished cry of "Kes!".

You have been killed by your best friend Mike.

## 90

You slap yourself in the face and speed up, a taste of blood in your mouth and agony screaming in your ankles, knees and hips you increase your pace to an unsustainable 7mph until after another twenty metres you inevitably suffer complete organ failure and nosedive into the grass verge stone dead.

Your adventure ends here.

## 91

Ushered on by a misguided confidence you walk down to the circle and force your way through the crowd, emerging in front of a surprised Peter Bones, who stares at you with a mixed expression of anger and more anger. He raises himself up to his freakish height, his face going crimson.

"Who the hell are you?" he bellows in a commanding voice that makes you confidence condense into a tiny fart that squeaks out of your bottom and dissipates. You begin to talk but your words catch in your throat, emerging from your mouth like a strange squeak, then you clear your throat and respond.

"I am Agravain Kestrel" you proclaim and stand there, surrounded by silence as your announcement washes over Peter and the crowd. You imagine the lack of reaction from the audience is because they are awed to have such a prominent YouTube star in their midst.

"Who?" says Peter Bones, destroying your fantasy but before you can answer he demands to know what you are doing here, a good question which takes you a while to answer.

"I am here as a guardian of culture." you start, surprised by your own eloquence "The world is fed up with your manufactured music, your sterile films and your ignorant, judgemental TV programs. I am here to put an end to the banality, no longer will you dictate who succeeds and who fails, people will rise to the top based on their individual talents, not relentless exposure and marketing." You stop talking and Peter smiles a wolfish grin.

"You alone are going to stop us?" he says mockingly, you laugh right back at him.

"Me and my reliable cameraman Mike! Say hello Mike." you reply, gesturing behind you to an empty space. "Mike?" you say as you look around wondering where he might have gone as Peter steps closer.

"Your flies are undone." he says in a loud voice, in horror you glance down at the gaping zip-hole and the whole circle erupts with laughter aimed directly at your crotch, it's like the school showers all over again.

You look back up from your groin and up at Peter as a long tongue flicks from between his teeth, he raises his eyebrows and there is a sudden glint in his eye which causes a flash of blinding, scorching light that instantly turns you into ash.

You are dead.

## 92

Regaining your composure, you casually take out your thread-bare Animal wallet. The last few functioning Velcro hooks make a barely inaudible tear as you open the wallet and remove your credit card. The chip and pin machine is swivelled viciously in your direction by the librarian and you reach forward, slotting your credit card into the bottom, then with great trepidation you type in your PIN number.

The next anxious five seconds feel like an eternity until, rather predictably, your card is declined. You try again and again, theatrically taking the card out and rubbing the chip and shaking your head. Each time the suspicion of the librarian increases until finally she taps a concealed button under her desk. Alarms blare out, red lights flash and reinforced shutters come crashing down over the exits. Panicking you flee through the shelves of books, banging off walls and changing directions randomly like Roomba. The librarian pulls out a taser and chases you, shouting obscene insults. You squat in the thriller section, tongue out, panting loudly with your knees screaming in agony as the crazed hunter stalks you. A protracted game of cat and mouse ensues until she finally corners you near the newspapers and due to a combination of poor aim and a last minute attempt by you to rush her, she unleashes 50,000 volts of electricity directly into your face.

You are dead (but have the funniest expression).

## 93

After what you can only assume has been several months in this cell without any food or drink you break down, mentally and physically you collapse. Visions of all of your favourite foods dance in front of your eyes, chips, jaffa-cakes, more chips. Your hand reaches out to grab these delicious treats but they are only cheeky hallucinations. Your mouth would drool if it had enough moisture.

Lying in a stupor and your own cold piss, you start to hear things. A distant voice calls your name and you laugh quietly in response, embracing your descent in madness.

"Kes! Kes!" The voice calls out once more and you roll over onto your side to face the door, giggling quietly.

Your steel yourself against the onset of psychological decline and go to sleep until someone comes and rescues you.

Turn to 125.

## 94

Assuming the owner of the phone has ordered something, you pick option 3 and are met by the same cold, hissing voice as before.

"Welcome field agent, your orders if you choose to accept are to infiltrate the Yorkshire Countrywoman's Association. Obviously if you are currently adopting a male human façade then you may need to kill off your current persona before altering your appearance." The voice then asks you to confirm if you are accepting this assignment by choosing 1 for yes or 2 for no.

Option 1, Yes you wish to accept this assignment (turn to 75)

Option 2, Err what? No thanks (turn to 66)

## 95

It's a ragtag selection in this library, there is no escaping it but without these CDs you'd have never truly discovered The Mavericks, Emmylou Harris or god forbid, Conway Twitty. Today you delve greedily into the CDs but its slim pickings, nothing you haven't heard before and some stuff you wish you hadn't.

Just as you are about to admit defeat and go home with an album of Willy Nelson covers you find the holy grail, a copy of the 1974 Dolly Parton album 'Love is like a butterfly' (presumably because it only lasts a day). You quickly snatch it off the shelf before anyone else gets it and rush home to study the front cover so fast you forget to check it out with the librarian.

Later that afternoon the window cleaner catches you wanking to the front cover whilst dressed as Kris Kristofferson and tells your neighbours. Your street cred in tatters you suffer for weeks as people shout 'Yipee Kay Aye' and 'Giddy up' as you walk around the neighbourhood – ultimately deciding to run away from home, ending up homeless on the streets of Manchester.

One bitter December evening a Deliveroo rider finds your frozen corpse lying in the road, clutching a Dolly Parton CD, but is working to such a strict deadline he only has time to snapchat the image to the police before cycling off and delivering his steaming, Thai cargo.


Your adventure ends here.


# 96

Struggling to see you walk straight forward into the road, oblivious to the oncoming lorry, the driver of which is currently sending a text. Looking up you notice the trucks radiator about a metre away from your face, when suddenly you are nudged clean out of its path. The lorry continues to cruise down the street leaving behind it a bloody mess on the cobbles, a crowd gather and you hear shocked voices mentioning the name Captain Jorvik. After some discussion it seems that you were indeed saved by York's own superhero, Captain Jorvik whose corpse is now smeared across the road like cherry jam on flapjack, his red cape mixing with the copious amounts of blood so that it's hard to see where his costume ends and the gore begins.

After an afternoon's soul searching you decide that Captain Jorvik's name must live on and decide the only way is for you to take on the mantel. After all, the original/dead guy was anonymous so nobody will know any different. That evening, wearing a hastily crafted costume made from fishnet stockings, a heavy maroon curtain, a red 'Hooty and the Blowfish' tee shirt and a children's Spiderman buff with eyeholes cut out of it, you take to the streets on the lookout for crime.

It rapidly gets cold and you get a bit bored, you consider stopping some drunk teenagers who are kicking in the front window to cash converters but decide that the insurance can sort that one. Within an hour you are home again and decide you have to plan this more thoroughly, however Mike has just bought a DVD box-set of Ren and Stimpy so you watch that instead. Despite your best intentions you never go out as Captain Jorvik again and his memory, much like his actual physical self, dies with you.

Your adventure ends here.

## 97

The bus is already at the bus-stop as you round the corner, forcing you to break into a pathetic half-run, the driver sees you, takes a moment to pity you and kindly waits. The driver immediately regrets his decision as you slowly count out the correct fare in five pence pieces before taking your seat. The bus is fairly busy yet you remain the only passenger under 60 years old, largely due to everyone else your age being at work. You dwell on this for a few seconds and remind yourself you have a higher calling, if you didn't investigate the dark corners of society and uncover the harsh truths of this world then who would? Nobody! That's who. Then what would happen?

Feeling like you have once again justified your unemployed status to the nagging voices of doubt in your head you stare out of the window and rapidly become under-stimulated. To stave off the approaching boredom you.

Try and count all of the yellow coloured cars you can see on the way to the job centre (turn to 69)

Rest your head against the window to feel the soothing vibrations of the buses diesel engine rumble through your skull (turn to 17)

## 98

In order to get clearer sound and therefore more incriminating evidence you suggest to Mike it would be wise to infiltrate the crowd and somehow work your way to the front. Mike conceals the camera within his lumberjack shirt and walks casually through the back end of the audience clutching his the fabric of his top awkwardly, making it look like he is cradling something small and camera shaped. Nobody challenges you or even seems to notice as you filter to the front of the baying throng, there is something strange about the people here. You subtly gawp at several people in the crowd and notice their eyes are yellow with black slits in place of pupils!

If you have the book 'Brainwashed' (turn to 73)

If you do not have the book 'Brainwashed and 'are thinking what the hell is this Brainwashed book, I've never heard anything about it' (turn to 100)

## 99

Five Pounds! Does York city council think you are a millionaire? If you had five pounds to spare you wouldn't be at the flipping library, you'd be, I don't know… well, probably buying some fast food, then once you've wasted your fiver you'd be back at the library I guess. You ask the battle axe behind the counter if she can lend you the money or if you can owe her it – she snorts derisively at both of your suggestions like a disapproving piglet.

If you want to leave with your chosen item you are going to have to somehow magic up five quid and the only possible way to do that would be to stick it on your credit card, but the 'never never' has taken a considerable battering in recent months and you are not sure if you even have the necessary 500 British pennies available to you. Of course you could always put it back – or nick it?

Whack it on the 'never-never' (turn to 92)

Get it on five-finger discount (turn to 47)

Admit that you are too poor to have nice things, put it back and go without (turn to 27)

## 100

Ignorant to what is happening, you push to the front of the crowd and watch Peter as he continues. You and Mike stands there looking like a couple of extremely sore thumbs and it is not long until Peter spots you. He can tell by your expression that you are confused and gestures to the audience for them to quieten down.

"You there" he says, pointing his finger, you look behind you, then realise he is pointing at you.

"What?" you respond with a certain lack of intelligence.

He asks what you are doing here and you say you don't really know, just had nowt else to do and you'd seen some stuff you couldn't explain so you followed the clues.

"Ahhh I'm afraid you have found out our little secret" explains Peter "Our little get together you have unwittingly gate-crashed is a secret club for very special people. To find us as you did, you must also be special, am I correct?" Well certainly for a time at school that is how the teachers referred to you so you agree with Peter, that you are in fact special.

"Then you must join us, special one." Peter decries "There is but one initiation ritual that must be observed first though, a drink from our goblet."

Peter walks towards you with, in his hands a silver goblet brims with a clear, bubbling liquid which looks very much like Sprite, a fizzy drink that would certainly make your top five list. You look towards Mike for guidance, but he seems to be well hidden in the crowd, what do you do?

Not since the LEGO club have you had a chance to be part of such a prestigious group, grab the goblet and chug (turn to 31)

You don't know the nature of this club, for all you know it could Caravanning! Also, the thought of sharing a goblet with all of these other people makes your OCD flare up. Reject the offer and

(turn to 8)

## 101

Not knowing what the name of the organisation is you go onto Facebook and write a post about the weird phone call you have had. Within minutes a not unpleasant vibration in your trouser pocket makes you aware that someone is trying to call you, looking at the screen you do not recognise the number but answer anyway, just glad to be wanted. After the call connects there is nothing but silence, you are used to these calls on your home phone number, no doubt a foreign voice will soon try to convince you that there is a problem with your windows computer and you aren't about to fall for that old trick, not for a fourth time anyway. You wait for the scammers voice but are surprised to hear laughter, very quiet at first but building into an unmistakeable evil cackle.

Turn to 121.

## 102

The phone beeps as you press one and some soothing classical hold music begins to play. Almost imperceptibly a hissing male voice melds with the mollifying melodies and your head begins to nod. Visions of comfy beds and fluffy pillows build inside your head as you feel your body begin to relax. Suddenly your hand holding the phone drops down away from your ear, yet the music and voices continue as you recline and begin float through the air on a cloud of loveliness.

Turn to 110.

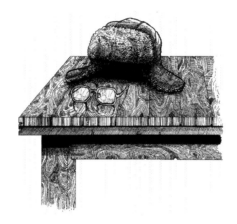

## 103

Without a further second thought you walk to the address on the card and find yourself in front of a Victorian, four storey town house. Bold as brass you skip up the stone steps, rap on the large black front door with your cane and wait.

"Who is it?" a voice on the other side of the door enquires. You clear your throat and announce that it is Agravain Kestrel, professional paranormal enthusiast.

"The prat off YouTube with the glasses and moustache?" the voice responds.

"That's me." you say enthusiastically and are promptly greeted with two, conjoined, hollow metal tubes that slide slowly through the letterbox and tilt upwards towards your face. Wondering what they are you stoop to inspect this strange object, realising all too late that it's a double-barrelled shotgun.

You are dead.

## 104

Mike's suggestion is like music to your ears, not just any music either – good music, like Billy Joel's masterpiece 'Innocent Man'. You've never been great in confined, dark places (or open, well-lit spaces come to think of it) so you latch onto Mike's arm and he begins to lead you back up towards the streets of York. Thankfully you encounter no resistance as you both traverse the winding tunnels leading back to the surface, but you notice Mike is becoming increasingly anxious, as if he has forgotten the way.

"Do you actually know where you're going?" you tactlessly ask Mike and he responds that he is adamant this is the way he came. Shining the torch downwards you can see he has scratched arrows on the floor however the corridor now ends in a dead end.

Mike doubles back with you in tow only to find the way you have just come is also now blocked by a stone wall. Each time the torch illuminates the end of the corridor you could swear that the walls are closer, yet they never seem to move. Suddenly the torch flickers and dims, you shake it frantically to reinvigorate the batteries (you've seen it done in movies) but accidentally let go and listen as it smashes against the encroaching stone wall that now stands ten feet away.

The darkness is terrible. You both walk a few paces with arms outstretched and quickly realise the end walls of the corridor are now somehow only 20 metres apart. Panic sets in. You go back and forth from dead end to dead end, the distance shortening each time until you find yourself able to touch both sides with each hand. Mike punches the wall ineffectively, you tut at his silly display of anger, then he punches you. Within minutes you both have standing room only, the air becomes close and warm and then you realise you don't even have room to turn you head.

Outside on the streets of York a shopper trying a sample of free fudge could swear she heard tortured screams as she bit into the rum raisin but puts it down to a recent course of antibiotics interfering with her anti-depressants.

You are dead.

## 105

Unprepared for such a philosophical question you launch headfirst into your response, not taking the time to run it past your brain.

"Monkeys!" you blurt out suddenly "That's how I got here, like all humans. Although I think it's actually apes, I dunno, which is the one with the tail? Anyway, before that all mammals have a common ancestor, like some sort of mouse or something. That's if you believe the scientists anyway." Peter stands in front of you, silent, mouth agape, so you continue "Unless of course you are more spiritual and believe in God or one of the Gods, there are lots of them and you can choose which one you want to be real, then fight against the others, sort of like picking your favourite sports team. Like when we were kids Mike used to really like the Legion of Doom and I liked The Rockers, you know with Shaun Michaels and the other one, what was his name? Oh yeah, Marty Jannetty. We were always arguing over who was the best tag team. Greg liked the Bushwhackers, I remember saying to him 'how can you like the Bushwhackers they are ridiculous'. Anyway, you know what I'm talking about, right, WWF? Not the World Wildlife Federation, that's the other WWF. I think the Wrestling one changed to WWE to stop the confusion. Mike, come here and we'll show Peter how to do the Boston Crab. Mike?" You look over to where

Mike was and he has vanished, you turn back to Peter in time to see a bag cover your face and with a heavy crack on the top of your head you hit the ground.

You are dead.

## 106

After you press the relevant button the English voice returns and announces it is 'taking you back to the main options'. For crying out loud!

Turn to 7.

## 107

The bottle smashes in Peter's face and he falls to the stone floor screaming and clutching his eyes. Around you the crowd begin falling to the ground convulsing, one by one, their yellow eyes rolling back into their skulls. Peter's screams seem to turn into a high-pitched screech as his skin peels back to reveal a rotting mass of green cartilage, the room quakes, huge pieces of masonry fall from the ceiling. Mike grabs your arm and you both quickly run out of the auditorium, climb the ladder and manage to find your back up through a maze of dark tunnels into the street, emerging into the daylight from a manhole cover in the middle of the city centre.

Over the course of the next few weeks you notice the quality of the music on the radio start to improve as the lingering spell of the Illuminati starts to dissipate. Previously lauded singers, actors and entertainers across the board are rounded up and destroyed for crimes against humanity. Worldwide culture begins to readjust and get back on track. MTV begins playing Grunge music again, BBC comedy programs become funny once more and most alarmingly of all film studios begin producing original, compelling stories and cancel all reboot cash ins.

Of course, being the modest person you are, you do not tell anyone about your involvement in the great culture shift, you know that now people are starting to think for themselves once more your reward will be a larger audience on YouTube and sure enough over the next six months you videos get another few hundred views.


Congratulations. You truly win!


Honestly - this is the best ending.

## 108

You burst from the Job Centre exit, barging through a crowd of loitering ne'er-do-wells, causing a heroin addict to spill his junk onto the pavement. A short but horrendously violent conflict occurs in which you are slaughtered in the most brutal way imaginable.

You are soooooo dead.

## 109

At the end of the corridor you find a wooden ladder that descends into a well-lit chamber, the cheering is clearly coming from there and to be honest you find it quite annoying. Mike leads the way down and you soon both find yourself in a huge underground, stone amphitheatre. Banners depicting an eye within a triangle hang from the walls. Forming a ring around the centre is a crowd of roughly two hundred spectators that seem to be the source of the clamour.

In the centre of the crowd you see four well-groomed young men dancing and singing, their voices are not audible over the din of the crowd. Suddenly the young men stop in a variety of poses and a spotlight swings around to highlight a tall man in a top hat, twirling a cane as he steps out into the centre.

"Silence!" screams the tall man as he strides towards the frozen wannabe boy band, "So what do we think?" Holding up his thumb the crowd start to cheer, the young men nervously relax and start to move when suddenly the tall man upends his thumbs and plunges it southwards.

The fervent crowd erupt and the confused performers are led away down a tunnel. The slender man silences the crowd once again, then removes his hat to reveal he is none other than Peter Bones from the popular TV program 'Ogre's Lair' – a curious program where members of the public have their earnest business ideas ridiculed and pulled apart by a group of fortunate businessmen for the entertainment of others.

"I'm afraid they didn't make the grade and as you all know, without our approval nothing can become popular in the mainstream culture" says Peter in a particularly on-the-nose piece of exposition. He holds out his hands and forms a triangular shape with them, then with a rasping noise from within his throat he shouts something incomprehensible, in unison every member of the crowd imitates Peter.

As you gormlessly stare at Peter, Mike begins to ready his camera, deleting several of your un-aired episodes in order to clear space on his memory card. He moves into position to get all of this evil on video, what do you do?

If you have the half eaten bag of jelly sweets from the cinema (turn to 16)

Tell Mike to hurry up and get the camera rolling so he doesn't miss anything (turn to 71)

Suggest you both get closer for a better view (turn to 98)

Stand up and issue a challenge to Peter like some sort of regular hero (turn to 91)

## 110

Your surroundings begins to feel unreal and you have a strange feeling of being pulled away from your body, confusion fills your mind as you realise you are in a dream.

Turn to 1.

## 111

The fancy dress shop doesn't have a chameleon costume but they do have a dragon costume and you figure this is sufficiently 'lizardy' so you decide to take it. Full payment is made when returning the costume but the lady behind the counter advises she needs a deposit. Thankfully she accepts your clothes as a suitable down payment and you leave the shop fully suited with just a short four mile walk to your destination.

Reaching the address on the card is easier said than done, the dragon costume's oversized feet make the journey ten times harder than usual, causing countless falls. Luckily the padding of the costume stops any serious injury but getting back up from the ground takes all your core strength. This exertion, including just moving forward causes the inside of the outfit to heat up until it smells like a styrofoam beef burger container, however despite the stench you finally reach an ominous looking four storey Victorian house, all windows have shutters over them and before you some stone steps lead to a large black door.

Why steps! Clearly the Victorian architect didn't take the possibility of someone having large foam feet into account when designing this entrance. You ascend clumsily and with great effort and like a contestant successfully scaling the travellator on Gladiators, you reach the top exhausted but chuffed.

The soft, silent knocking from your oversized, padded hand doesn't manage to bring anyone to the door, but by craning your head you manage to spy a doorbell through

the tiny eyeholes. Extending out one chunky digit your press the button but hear nothing apart from the clunk of a large brass nozzle that has appeared above the doorway. Suddenly the nozzles sprays out a foul smelling blue liquid that eats into the costume and burns your eyes, within seconds the outfit has dissolved and the caustic substance begins to melt through your skin, muscle and bones.

You are dead.

# 112

Nine minutes of lucid, anxious dreams pass by in a heartbeat until your alarm clock shrieks you back into consciousness. Your fist comes down onto the snooze button at an awkward angle, hurting the fleshy part of your hand near the base of your thumb.

Cursing the pain in your hand you sit up to check your phone and knock a glass of water across the bedside table, soaking your copy of The DaVinci Code. Running to the bathroom to get some toilet paper you catch your little toe on one of the bed legs, bending it to an unnatural ninety-degree angle and double up in pain. By the time you've finished faffing about you have well and truly missed any chance you ever had of making your appointment at the job centre so you just stand there in the middle of your bedroom, paralysed with thought. You make the mistake of glancing at your middle aged body in the mirror and feel a black depression approaching like a storm cloud, this day is rapidly becoming un-salvageable, what do you do?

Go to the place where logic and reason rule, where all opinions are considered valid and every man treats his fellow man with re-spect... the Internet (turn to 55)

Give up and go back to bed hoping tomorrow brings solutions in-stead of problems (turn to 51)

Just get dressed and get out of the house (turn to 123)

## 113

Preparation is key, so whilst you wait for Mike to come home you eat four bags of Wotsits and play minesweeper. Eventually Mike returns from whatever it is he does with his day, work or something and he crashes down on the sofa shattered. Almost immediately he is into his first beer, so you decide to ask him now before the inevitable nightly cloud of drunken misanthropy descends upon him. He thinks it's a stupid idea and thinks you are barking up the wrong tree, you disagree, you both argue and you storm off upstairs crying. After twenty minutes and an extremely upset entry in your diary the thought occurs that Mike is not required, only his camera is. Besides it might be pleasant to do an investigation without his constant sarcastic, mumbled comments.

Mike doesn't notice as you sneak out of the back door, he doesn't even look away from Top Gear when you loudly shout that you are just popping out for a few hours adding "Not got your camera or anything!" to avoid suspicion.

Having escaped from the will-sapping pall of your best friend you feel a renewed enthusiasm as you follow your phones GPS to the postcode on the card, soon finding yourself on a dimly lit Victorian street. The house in question stands silently at the bottom of the road, windows shuttered, stone steps leading up to an ominous looking black front door. Un-bagging the camera you turn it on and point it towards yourself to begin the episode, humming the theme tune before speaking. Gradually as you present to the camera you get the impression that you are at home, watching this on your computer; glancing around the air feels close and a loud beeping noise fills your ears.

Turn to 1.

## 114

The card feels so luxurious, it is clearly a step above the Kestrel Investigates business cards you got free from Vistaprint. Underneath the establishments name is white print of a Chameleon's skull. Flipping over the card over you see the club's address with the instructions 'ring bell', a phone number is scrawled in pen and with the words 'Call first – Lacerta-Smythe'. You recognise the name Lacerta-Smythe as being the double-barrelled surname of your local Conservative MP Henry Lacerta-Smythe, but why would he be leaving message inside a DVD case in the library? Your curiosity piques and you decide to find out more about this clandestine club.

Save your phone credit and go to the address on the card (turn to 119)

Risk taking the bait and call the number as instructed (turn to 18)

## 115

The crowd looks feverish as they jostle each other trying to peek a glimpse of their deity. Sidling over to the counter you make your opinion known to Creepy Conrad in a lowered voice to minimise the risk of confrontation with the clamouring fans. Conrad nods and thoughtfully puffs on his inhaler as he considers your argument, his eyes darting wildly he answers with an obvious sense of duress claiming that you are overreacting.

It is clear that some outside influence is at work here, Conrad is no stranger to pedantry yet today he seems reluctant to engage in discussion, you refuse to believe this is the same man who once argued for three straight hours that Krull was set in the same universe as Dune.

Accept that in order to flourish 'Journeyman' needs to widen its audience to the proles and leave the shop (turn to 19)

Keep talking to Creepy Conrad but start winking occasionally to signal that you know he is being monitored (turn to 33)

Join the great unwashed and queue to speak to Russell Bland yourself (turn to 24)

## 116

Putting your hand in your coat's left pocket you fish around until you remember that you put the potion in the other pocket. Pulling out the bottle of thick, brown liquid Peter notices you are free and runs towards you with his arms outstretched. You initially think he wants a hug but something about the obscenities he is shouting makes you think he is in a more aggressive mood, you have to think fast, what do you do?

Quickly drink the contents of the bottle before Peter can reach you (turn to 86)

Panic and throw the bottle at Peter (turn to 107)

## 117

Happy, prosperous members of the public wander past you (and in one case through you) as you stand in the middle of the large room looking pathetic. Eventually a woman leading a group of adults with learning difficulties enquires if you have lost somebody. She takes your blank stares and quiet mumbling as a yes and checks with a member of staff to see if they saw you come in with anyone. Unwilling to leave you alone she insists you to join her group to go and watch an animated children's film called 'Nuts', a heart-warming film about a plucky young squirrel who wants to make it as a YouTuber which turns out to be not only a genuine tearjerker but also contains some real tips on how to get noticed on such a crowded platform. Shortly after the film finishes you duck out whilst the kind lady is performing the Heimlich manoeuvre on one of her group, hiding in the toilet then wandering into the next showing of the Bond film.

Turn to 38.

## 118

The warm glowing feeling coursing through your body makes you feel happy, a clear indicator that something is out of the ordinary. Remembering Mother Gaia's potion and her warning that you would 'know when to use it' you wonder if it could somehow reverse the effect of the drink you have just imbibed. Every touch against your skin makes you feel ecstatic and as you fish around in your pockets you nudge the tip of your willy, making you sink to your knees in orgasmic pleasure. It's now or never you think and open Mother Gaia's bottle, guzzling its thick contents down like a Maccy D's milkshake. You wait, shuddering on your knees until the potion reaches your belly, Peter watches in morbid curiosity. Suddenly your stomach gurgles loudly and the golden haze of your surroundings falls away, you roll onto your side as your stomach begins to visibly swell and your bottom sputters with loud flatulence. Quickly your anal trumpeting become continuous, your tummy now begins to rip the waistline of your trousers as it continues to grow at an accelerated rate. Everyone in the room begins to back off as every part of your body swells, you look down to your hand and it looks like an inflated rubber glove. The pressure behind your eyes builds until you can no longer see, all you can hear is the sound of blood rushing and it fills your hearing like the roar of a mighty ocean. Holes begin to appear in your skin, slight tears in the surface venting off excess gas but the main bulk of your body increases until, finally, reaching your critical psi, you explode like a blood-filled balloon.

You are dead.

## 119

The address on the card is not a part of York you recognise so you Google it on Bing. Nothing significant comes up, it just seem like an everyday street and not the sort of place you would find a club, unless it was a working men's club … but let's hope it's not.

Now, you have to be very careful how to approach this situation because it's clear that the Chameleon Club is trying to remain secret and if you go blundering in then they might not appreciate it, what should you do?

Go blundering in (turn to 103)

Take the name literally and go hire a Chameleon outfit from the fancy-dress shop before heading to the address (turn to 111)

Go home, wait for Mike and then go make an episode investigating the strange address (turn to 113)

## 120

The cheers fill a hole inside of you that you didn't know existed, a lust for fame and celebrity status that can only be sated by the adoring public. It dawns on you that this was why you made your web-series all along, not to find cryptozoological creatures or extra-terrestrials, simply to massage your ego.

Over the next few months Peter and his cronies help your show go from strength to strength, incorporating celebrity guests and musical acts into your fifteen minute YouTube videos. You are the next big thing and everything is great for fifteen series. By this time the public no longer see you as a novelty, you have become a brand with Kestrel tee shirts, hats, watches, action figures and even a Kestrel cereal. You lose interest, the shows stop, Peter Bones invites you into the top echelons of The Illuminati and you become 'influential'.

Your life now consists of being photographed at events, appealing for people to donate to charities and a habitual addiction to strong painkillers.

You win (sort of).

## 121

You try to hang up but to your horror the phone is somehow stuck to your hand by some unseen force, almost like strong magnetism. The phone begins to heat up until your skin is burning. A high pitched whistling noise begins to emanate from the phones speakers and the handset grows unbearably hot until it finally explodes, the shrapnel from the metal case lacerates your arm, torso, face and neck, slicing through your carotid artery, sending pulsing jets of bright red blood ten feet in front of you. You try and stem the blood with your hand but the explosion has turned then end of your arm into what looks like a burst cigar. A member of the public asks if you are alright and worries alongside you as you expire, then they steal your hat.

You are dead.

## 122

Wiping the blood from your face you stroll through the pictur-esque streets of York with a sense of achievement. Obviously you would rather not have been forced to steal your prize and you certainly would have loved to avoid being beaten up but, hey ho, life is like a box of chocolates, in your case a shit box of chocolates. Walking along the shambles, past the endless parade of wizarding shops you become paranoid that the security guard is following you, glancing back you are sure you see his piggy face in the crowd and speed up, darting down snickets and up ginnels. Panting heavily you stop behind a restaurant to catch your breath, seven minutes pass by and you begin to walk slowly and cautiously down another alleyway. As your head pops out into the street a heavy blow to the top of your head sends your world spinning – everything fades to black.

Turn to 56.

## 123

Closing the front door you step out into the fresh morning air and instantly feel better for it. An old man dodders along the pavement with a folded up, far-right broadsheet newspaper under his armpit.

"Morning." he croaks as he passes you by. You suspect the old man to be a Brexiteer and reluctantly respond, the fresh air has raised your spirits so much that not even the UK's impending economic disaster can dampen your mood. You set off with a spring in your step and stone in your shoe not knowing where your bowed legs might carry you.

If you wish to go to the Library to rub shoulders with students and unemployed graduates (turn to 20)

If you want to see which selection of superhero films is currently playing at the cinema (turn to 14)

If you want to use your phone to enslave virtual animals on the new augmented reality app 'Jabaguy Go' (turn to 60)

## 124

As you enter Journeyman the delicious smell of brand new comics and adult comics (graphic novels) is quickly soured as you realise what the queue is for. Lounging at a table, chest hair bursting from a low-cut, V-neck tee-shirt sits TV presenter Russell Bland. The vapid waste of human material is promoting the comic book adaptation of his autobiography 'My Story Wory'. Rage fills every corner of your flabby body as you realise this figurehead of mainstream rubbish has successfully managed to sully your bastion of nerd culture. You feel unhinged, dangerous, a man on the edge. What do you do, I mean what can YOU do?

Leave the shop and scrunch the white-hot anger coursing through your veins into a little ball so it can be dealt with through your own unique form of self-flagellation later i.e. by watching The Big Bang Theory or gorging on Greggs sausage rolls (turn to 29)

Join the queue in order to personally deliver an insult to Mr Bland and hope that your anger doesn't dissipate before you reach him (turn to 24)

Speak to your friend Creepy Conrad who is currently cowering behind the counter and demand that he tell you how on God's green, flat Earth this travesty has occurred (turn to 115)

## 125

Each time you awake you feel weaker and soon you are desperate with hunger and thirst, you begin to realise that you have been left here to die. You try in vain to break down the door but successfully break your shoulder. The tears stroll down you face and you greedily lick them up.

Over the course of a few weeks your body expires, and you steadily rot on the cell floor.

Two thousand years in the future an alien race discover your remains and display them in a museum as a perfect example of human female.

You are dead.

# ACKNOWLEDGEMENT

A huge thankyou to Anthony Farren for the front cover and the many excellent posters and images he produces for Kestrel Investigates, Miles Watts for always helping me develop ideas, Jon Procter for his incredible illustrations and finally my wife Helen for her unwavering support.

# ABOUT THE AUTHOR

## Oliver Semple

An academic failure, Oliver Semple is the youngest of four siblings. Early on in life it occurred to him that to be noticed within the household he would need a gimmick, something that set him apart, so like many other nervous, defensive people before him, he decided he would try and develop a sense of humour.

It wasn't until graduating from Hull with a 2:2 in Fine Art that Oliver turned his limited abilities to writing. For several years he co-owned and operated a comedic comic called Lobster, in which he vented his fury and angst through a strip called John Alone.

After being hit by a car Oliver moved from Hull to York and after a few years of writing and planning co-wrote and produced a feature film called Kenneth, released in 2012 to a smattering of praise.

At the back end of 2017 Kestrel Investigates was born and Oliver has written, filmed and acted in two full series, with a third series and feature film in the works alongside other projects.

Printed in Poland
by Amazon Fulfillment
Poland Sp. z o.o., Wrocław